THE MOON CRUISE

THE MOON CRUISE

ESMIE JIKIEMI-PEARSON

BBC Books, an imprint of Ebury Publishing

UK | USA | Canada | Ireland | Australia
India | New Zealand | South Africa

BBC Books is part of the Penguin Random House group of companies whose addresses can be found at global.penguinrandomhouse.com

Penguin Random House UK
One Embassy Gardens, 8 Viaduct Gardens, London SW11 7BW

penguin.co.uk
global.penguinrandomhouse.com

First published by BBC Books in 2025

1

Copyright © Esmie Jikiemi-Pearson 2025
The moral right of the author has been asserted.

Penguin Random House values and supports copyright. Copyright fuels creativity, encourages diverse voices, promotes freedom of expression and supports a vibrant culture. Thank you for purchasing an authorised edition of this book and for respecting intellectual property laws by not reproducing, scanning or distributing any part of it by any means without permission. You are supporting authors and enabling Penguin Random House to continue to publish books for everyone. No part of this book may be used or reproduced in any manner for the purpose of training artificial intelligence technologies or systems. In accordance with Article 4(3) of the DSM Directive 2019/790, Penguin Random House expressly reserves this work from the text and data mining exception.

Doctor Who is produced in Wales by Bad Wolf with BBC Studios Productions. Executive Producers: Jane Tranter, Julie Gardner, Joel Collins, Phil Collinson and Russell T Davies.

Typeset by Six Red Marbles UK, Thetford, Norfolk

Printed and bound in Great Britain by Clays Ltd, Elcograf S.p.A.

The authorised representative in the EEA is Penguin Random House Ireland, Morrison Chambers, 32 Nassau Street, Dublin D02 YH68

A CIP catalogue record for this book is available from the British Library

ISBN 9781785949777

Penguin Random House is committed to a sustainable future for our business, our readers and our planet. This book is made from Forest Stewardship Council® certified paper.

To my sisters

Contents

Chapter One	1
Chapter Two	15
Chapter Three	27
Chapter Four	41
Chapter Five	53
Chapter Six	63
Chapter Seven	75
Chapter Eight	85
Chapter Nine	95
Chapter Ten	103
Chapter Eleven	113
Chapter Twelve	127
Chapter Thirteen	141
Chapter Fourteen	157
Chapter Fifteen	167
Chapter Sixteen	181
Acknowledgements	191

Chapter One

The TARDIS slammed into the ground with all the grace of a brick hurled at someone's face. Sparks skittered across the floor of the control room, alarms blared and died, then blared again. Belinda Chandra found herself in total disarray, limbs flying, hair in her face, sliding across the floor. Or was it the ceiling?

The TARDIS rattled one last time, and was still.

'Brace yourself for landing . . .' the Doctor called. He was standing by the console, a perfect picture of composure in a matchy orange outfit that reminded her of a kurta, but shorter. Over the top, he wore a gorgeous dark red vest that fell to mid-thigh. All of it was creaseless and pressed; the only hint that he had just been thrown through time and space was the giddy glint in his eyes, which she noticed he got whenever they landed somewhere new.

Belinda picked herself up from the floor one limb at a time, her glare so caustic it could have stripped paint. 'A little late for that, don't you think?'

The Doctor held his hands up in mock surrender. Silver rings glinted on his fingers. 'Sorry.'

Belinda shook her head. The longer they travelled together, the more she began to suspect he liked the chaos. Thrived in it, perhaps. 'No, you're not.'

His smiled widened. 'I am so.'

Brushing dust off her knees, Belinda stood. 'Look, just go and get your Vindicator, so we can get the reading, and get out. Please?'

That's why they had landed here, on an asteroid in the middle of nowhere, in the twenty-seventh century. The Vindicator needed more readings before it could anchor back to the fateful date of 24 May 2025. But nearly every time they'd landed prior to this, they'd been carried off on some mad adventure. The things they'd seen! A god of light in Miami, 1952. Telepathic fungi and a living spacecraft. A colony base on a barren world, its crew stalked by an ancient, malevolent creature. She'd almost died. A shudder went down her spine at the memory.

After that, Belinda had specifically requested they land in the most boring place the Doctor could think of in all of time and space, so he'd chosen this. An empty stretch of galaxy, populated by ... rocks!

Rocks are good. Nice and boring, Belinda had agreed. *Let's go there.*

'Hey Belinda.' The Doctor appeared behind her, the Vindicator slung by its strap over one arm, so that he looked like a popstar with his guitar. 'Sorry about that *rocky* landing. Ha! Got to love them, though.'

'I don't.' She whirled round, coming face to face with him. Her hip ached where it had smashed against the bottom of the console, and her ears were ringing. 'I love the idea of getting home, Doctor. I love the idea of hearing my mum play the violin again, or . . . or karaoke nights with my dad. I like the idea of a warm, comforting home-cooked meal, and *my own bed*. What if I never get to have that again?'

For just a moment, a shadow passed across the Doctor's expression. But then he smiled again. 'Is my cooking really that bad?'

Despite herself, Belinda felt an answering smile tug at her mouth. 'Doctor, you put tinned sardines on a piece of chocolate and called it dinner.'

His brow furrowed. 'Salt and sweet. What's wrong with that?'

Belinda walked past him before he could see her smiling in earnest. It was ridiculous, how charming he was. How quickly he could turn her mood around. She wondered if he'd had lots of practice, assuaging the fears of grumpy human beings. She knew there had been others before her – other people who had travelled with the Doctor. She got the sense they'd all been a bit more wide-eyed and in love with it all. Sometimes, she understood that. But she had a life back in London, one she very much wanted to return to alive. She walked to the door, resting her palm on it, before turning back to the Doctor, who was mumbling something about *the limited human palate*.

She leaned against the door, pushing on it gently. 'May I?'

'Be my guest,' he nodded.

Belinda grinned, and pushed open the door.

She'd expected views for miles – the empty vacuum of space stretching on, speckled with diamond-like stars – suns, really – and the billowing clouds of gas and dust called nebulae, where stars were born. She'd secretly wanted to see a comet, one like Halley's comet, with a bright tail of light, or a passing spaceship, crawling through the darkness.

The sight that greeted her was totally underwhelming. A concrete corridor stretched out for many yards, strange symbols painted on it in reflective paint. One of them looked like a stick-figure of some strange life form getting electrocuted by jagged bolts of lightning. Her heart stopped. She wondered if she should turn back, go back to the TARDIS and demand the Doctor redo his calculations, remove them from this time and place and try again. She was hit with a strange pang of homesickness. She missed her room in the house share, her housemates taking too long in the bathroom. She missed the hospital – the routines, and the training, the way she had always known what to do, even if she felt overwhelmed.

Beside her, the Doctor stepped out of the TARDIS, Vindicator hefted over one shoulder. 'Oh.'

'Not an asteroid.'

'Definitely not an asteroid.' He took a few brash steps forward, drawing the sonic out of an inside pocket and scanning the walls. Its high-pitched whine had become comforting. Usually, the sonic meant *answers*. But now the Doctor frowned, holding the sonic close to his eyes to read it better in the low, flickering light of the corridor. 'But that doesn't make any sense,' he muttered.

'What doesn't?'

'We are in a very, very large building.' He turned the sonic upside down and squinted at it. 'And we're moving, but not along an orbital path . . .' He paused, eyes darting around. 'Can you hear that?'

Belinda listened hard. Nothing. Or . . . was that a faint rumble?

The Doctor caught her eye and nodded. 'Engines. Which means we are on a ship.' He rattled off some calculations under his breath. 'But we're travelling slowly. *Leisurely.*'

'Maybe the ship's broken down,' said Belinda. 'Can we still get a reading from the Vindicator?'

'We can, but it will take longer. It's better to take readings in the open air, outside, without any concrete or metal in the way, blocking the signal.'

Belinda looked around. The corridor seemed clean and normal. At the end of it was a set of double doors, a circular window in each door. White light glowed through them, bright as daylight. There was something comforting about it. In the silence, punctuated only by the Doctor's mutterings, Belinda thought she could hear music. Fairground music, with piping trumpets and clashing cymbals. Very far away, was the sound of someone laughing. Something in the corridor caught her eye – it was next to the TARDIS, half hidden in its shadow. That was why she hadn't noticed it before. Walking past the still-muttering Doctor, Belinda reached out a hand. It was a banner, half drooped over and curled in on itself like a dead insect. Hesitantly, her fingers brushed against the papery material. It was soft and luxurious feeling, though a thick layer of soft, grey dust coated her fingers. The banner was long – it took several paces for her to unroll it, smoothing it back up against the wall. The old glue caught and held, for just a moment. Long enough for her to read the message embossed across it in thick gold letters.

WELCOME TO THE MAIDEN VOYAGE
OF THE MOON CRUISE!

Behind her, the Vindicator dropped to the floor with a thud. She whirled round.

The Doctor was staring at the message. His eyes were wide, his face was filled with childish glee. 'Oh, I never thought I'd see the day,' he breathed. He turned back to the TARDIS, resting his hand on it. 'You cheeky thing.'

'Doctor, what is it?'

The Moon Cruise

'Sometimes, the TARDIS meddles.' He put the Vindicator down, unfolded it and set it up. With a final press of a button, it glowed blue. Casting its signal out, trying to find 2025. Then he laughed. 'You've been so stressed out, Bel. I think she sensed it, and wanted to help.'

'By taking us on a cruise?' Belinda asked.

'Not any old cruise.' He strode off, towards the double doors at the end of the corridor. Belinda ran to catch up, a million questions on her mind. But when the Doctor reached the doors and pushed them open, all her questions faded away.

Infinite levels of glass and marble stretched upwards and downwards, connected by enormous staircases that spiralled from floor to floor, their golden steps lit up like runways. There must have been hundreds of floors, all of them gleaming with luxury finishes: marbled stone bannisters and lush red carpets. In the centre, an art installation made of hanging titanium cables was dotted with cut-out chrome stars and glittering planets with elaborate rings – emphasising the 'space cruise' theme. On the floor opposite them, a restaurant bustled with activity, smartly dressed waiters weaving in between hundreds of round, white-clothed tables, as families of all types ate and drank, laughing as their cutlery flashed and glasses *clinked* merrily. The biggest buffet table Belinda had ever seen stretched from one end of the dining area to the other. It was stacked dizzyingly high with roasted meats and vegetables, gleaming piles of brightly coloured fruits, and seafood on ice. A dessert table overflowed with towering cakes and creams, a multi-tiered extravaganza that made her mouth water just looking at it.

Another wide-eyed look across the balcony revealed an intriguing fact: humans weren't the only patrons on board the space cruise. A myriad of different people, hailing from planets all around the galaxy, had come to enjoy this life of leisure. Belinda took a step back to make way as a family of four walked in front of them, each carrying enormous disposable cups of fizzy drinks, with shopping bags weighing down all seven of their tentacular arms.

'Welcome to the Moon Cruise,' the Doctor said, sweeping one hand in a broad arc across the view. 'The largest cruise that ever attempted to cross this galaxy. As famous as the *Titanic* was on Earth, the Moon Cruise will go down in history as one of the most ambitious leisure voyages in history. You are standing on the biggest spaceship built for several centuries.'

'You're telling me that the TARDIS thought I needed to *relax*, so it brought us to the *Titanic* in space?'

'But the Moon Cruise never wrecked, Belinda! It disappeared.' At her expression of horror, he elaborated. 'But only for fifty years. I do know for certain that the cruise docked back safely on its home planet, after seventy years total of voyaging. A lot had changed on board between the time it had left and its reappearance. But there were no fatalities. Just a bit of a mystery.' He waggled his eyebrows. 'And you know how I feel about mystery. Ah!' he exclaimed. 'A map.' To his left, there was a short podium, labelled with a big silver button, and a map icon. Belinda tilted her head, confused, until the Doctor pressed the button and a hologram buzzed to life. In front of them hovered a miniature model of a spaceship. On the side, enormous letters read: MOON CRUISE INC.

'We're standing inside that,' the Doctor murmured. Belinda felt a rush of vertigo at the idea. It was hard to judge the scale of the spacecraft. Thousands of windows glittered on its sides as the craft moved steadily through space, and there must have been hundreds of levels. The craft was curiously similar to a seafaring vessel; it was shaped like the enormous cargo ships that carried thousands of shipping containers across the sea – long, but bulky, with a pointy bow and a blunt stern, where the engines' exhaust nozzles glowed softly.

The Doctor swiped his hand over the hologram. It swivelled at his command, spinning slowly so that Belinda could see every angle of it. Labels had started to pop up all over the ship, including one that said, *You're here*. The ship grew narrower toward the lower decks, which Belinda noticed were unlabelled. Maybe they were off limits.

According to the *You're here* label, they were standing near the front, on the bow if it had been a regular ship. Leaning forward, Belinda reached out and tapped the words labelling their location. To her delight, the hologram zoomed in, whizzing past all the different amenities – spas, shopping malls, cinemas and . . . was that *mini-golf?* – until they saw two tiny avatars standing on the same walkway they stood on, surrounded by blinking arrows pointing in a thousand different directions. *Turn right for the pickleball courts, left for the flower-arranging workshop, or straight on for the chocolatier experience.*

Belinda's eyes widened. 'How long does the Vindicator need?'

'Here?' The Doctor shrugged. 'Well, given the safety shielding . . . maybe a few hours.'

'A few hours . . .' Her mind was racing – had they actually hit the destination jackpot? The thought of going to a spa, eating a meal that wasn't whipped up by the Doctor or herself, was incredible, and so tantalisingly close. She looked longingly at the buffet. What could it hurt? To let loose a little bit on the biggest cruise in the galaxy?

A woman walked past, wearing a beautiful dress. It was sleek and chromatic, with ruffles at the wrists and a thousand colours dancing across the beaded skirt. Belinda stared after her, watching her sashay into a fashion boutique, where mannequins in outrageously luxurious outfits posed demurely behind glass. *Wow.* Between her nurse scrubs and her favourite pair of joggers, Belinda could count on one hand the number of times she'd had the opportunity to put on a nice dress, or a pair of fancy shoes. Most of the time back home, she could convince herself she didn't care – that it was vapid, or shallow, to care too much about her appearance. But the rush it had given her when the TARDIS clothed her in that fabulous yellow dress when they'd landed in 1952 had reminded her that she did care. Besides, the TARDIS had been choosing her outfits for ages now. She was a grown woman, not a toddler. If she wanted to try on a few things in the boutiques, sample the fashion from whatever crazy far-future century they had wound up in, how could anyone object to that?

'Doctor—'

'I know,' he interrupted, his voice grave. 'I know what you're going to say. After all I've put you through, we should stay put, stay close to the TARDIS and stay out of trouble.' He nodded, eyes serious. 'And for you, I'll do it.'

'Slow down, Doctor,' Belinda said, grinning. 'What I was *going to say* was ... after everything we've been through, a bit of retail therapy wouldn't go amiss.' She shrugged, a little giddy at the thought of just how *much* there was to explore on board the Moon Cruise. 'If the Vindicator needs a few hours, then maybe we can explore a bit. Browse the shops, maybe find a souvenir or two to take home ... ?' She trailed off, looking at him hopefully.

For a moment his expression remained grave, but the twinkle in his eyes gave him away before his smile did. 'I thought you'd never ask.' Before she knew it, the Doctor had grabbed her hand, laughing as he pulled her away from the TARDIS and into the bright lights of the ship's dazzling interior.

Chapter Two

Belinda sat in a comfy chair, sighing in relief as a masseuse squeezed every last bit of tension from her shoulders. She had a face mask on that smelled like cucumber, mint and something she couldn't identify. The mask left her face tingling, as though it were being tapped by a thousand tiny fingertips. Her feet were in comfy slippers, propped up on a low stool, and she had a glass of something cold, fizzy and delicious in her hand. She couldn't remember the last time she'd treated herself to anything like this. It was perfect, and tranquil. So lovely, she could almost drop off to sleep.

'My face is tingling,' the Doctor whispered loudly, breaking her reverie.

'Shush. That means it's working.'

Opposite them, a TV was playing. On the screen, a blonde woman clad in a pinstriped skirt suit was talking to the host of a breakfast show.

'The Moon Cruise is my pride and joy,' she beamed. Her lipstick was perfect: perfect shape, perfect red. Her eyes were large and blue, fringed with dark lashes. 'I've worked so hard over the years to create a place that truly feels like a home away from home. We are a mere six years into the voyage, with a predicted total sailing duration of thirty years, so I am aware it is early days. However, the feedback has been phenomenal, and so I think we can be cautiously optimistic that the maiden voyage of the ship will be a resounding success.' She was mesmerising to look at. The host of the show nodded, a simpering smile taking over her face at the woman's words.

'Who is that?' Belinda asked the masseuse.

The woman's hands paused for a moment. 'That's Marilyn Moon,' she answered stiffly. 'She created the cruise. She comes from a big shipping family, but she's tripled the company's profits since launching the cruise.' Another pause. In the reflection of the window, Belinda saw her look at her colleague. They exchanged a look that Belinda could not decipher. *Worry?* Or perhaps a look of encouragement, for the masseuse cleared her throat and said quickly, 'Marilyn is amazing. All of us on the cruise, we just want to make her proud.' The masseuse took a step back and removed her gloves. 'Will that be all for today?'

After the spa, they went to the restaurant. Belinda loaded up her plate with something from every bowl – stews and crusty bread with butter, roasted vegetables glazed with honey and salt, the fluffiest mashed potatoes and a quiche that melted in her mouth. Dessert was strawberry ice cream and chocolate cake, then a mango milkshake, and three chocolate chip cookies straight from the oven.

Yawning, and full to the brim, they walked around the retail floors – which were endless, like the biggest shopping centre Belinda had ever been to. They passed bookstores, and Belinda dragged the Doctor into candle shops so they could sniff every single one. They wandered into the jewellery store, where Belinda convinced the Doctor to try on an elegant pair of diamond and emerald earrings. They posed with handbags in the boutiques, took photos in silly scarves inside an old-fashioned photo booth and pretended to be serious shoppers while trying on fancy watches in a shop where every single surface was covered in dark leather. Perfumes were spritzed and sampled, and Belinda had to drag the Doctor away from one shop after she accidentally upended an entire bottle of body glitter onto a white carpet. They ran to the arcade, an endless dark floor filled with games. They threw balls into hoops and won stuffed animals of species that Belinda had never seen before. They raced motorbikes inside a virtual reality, and played each other's avatars at tennis in a Grand Slam tournament.

Belinda sat down on a bench in a small alcove, her shoulders shaking with laughter. 'Oh my *goodness*, I can't believe how much fun this is.' She felt lighter than she had in months, and giddy with new experiences. 'This cruise is incredible. I can't believe I wanted to land on an asteroid when places like this exist. When we get back to the TARDIS I am going to give the console a hug, because I *so* needed this.'

The Doctor checked the time. 'Well, we should be getting back. The Vindicator should have retrieved its data by now.'

Belinda spotted something across the way, and gasped. 'Oh, but Doctor, look! A souvenir shop.' She smiled. 'I want something to remember this by.'

The Doctor stood up and bowed, gesturing to the storefront. 'Your wish is my command, Miss Chandra.'

The souvenir shop was far bigger than it seemed from the outside.

This was to be their final stop on the cruise – the last place they visited before going back to the TARDIS, collecting the Vindicator and leaving. Belinda wasn't even sure she knew what she wanted as a souvenir. Luckily, the shop was crammed with options. T-shirts were folded into towers, with the many mottos of the Moon Cruise emblazoned across them: ESCAPE YOUR HORIZONS! FUN STARTS AMONG THE STARS! I WENT ON THE LONGEST CRUISE IN THE GALAXY AND ALL I GOT WAS THIS T-SHIRT. Belinda laughed to herself, and picked that one up, tucking it into her basket. She walked past walls of keychains adorned with tiny planets and shooting stars caked in glitter. A shelf of Marilyn Moon bobble heads nodded at her, as she ducked into one of the many aisles displaying postcards from different planets on the Moon Cruise route. She picked up a postcard from a planet with several colourful moons, the words WISH YOU WERE HERE! emblazoned across them.

'Feed me!' chirped a robotic voice. Belinda jumped, looking towards the source of the noise. Next to the biggest display was a small robot. It was bright yellow, with a long rectangular slot on its face underneath the two flashing cubes that formed its eyes.

'Aw. Aren't you adorable,' Belinda said, resting her hands on her knees as she bent down closer to the bot.

'Feed me!' the robot repeated. She raised an eyebrow, only to see the words POSTBOT emblazoned across its chest. 'Feed me!' *Ah.* This little bot must be how they sent mail off the cruise. She had assumed it worked in the same way as a regular cruise – the passengers would disembark and post them at each stop across the galaxy. But on reflection, it was difficult enough to post something from a different country, let alone a different planet. And the fees ... she shuddered to imagine the cost of sending a postcard to *another planet*. This was far simpler, as the postbot's label explained: FEED YOUR POSTCARD TO THE BOT, AND YOUR LOVED ONES BACK HOME WILL RECEIVE A HIGH-QUALITY SCAN!

Belinda wondered what would happen if she fed a postcard to the bot, and typed in her parents' email address. Probably nothing exciting enough to warrant the risk of being found out, she thought. So she moved on, strolling past the T-shirts, but regret twinged in her heart. Her family had a longstanding tradition of always picking one kitschy, silly item per person to bring back from a trip – whether it was a funny fridge magnet, or a particularly hideous postcard, they always made sure to do it. She paused, picking up a bulky magnet in the shape of the ship. Its boat shape fitted comfortably in the palm of her hand, its endless decks and tiny windows recreated in miniature. The magnet was emblazoned with the words THE GALAXY'S BIGGEST ADVENTURE. It felt apt, the words describing how she'd been feeling ever since she started travelling with the Doctor. She rubbed her thumb over the ridges of it. If she told them about everything that had happened ... would they even believe her?

Shaking her head, she slipped the magnet into her pocket and moved on.

At the back of the shop were four huge towering displays of sunglasses – one tower for each number of eyes on the glasses. The cruise had to cater to lots of clientele with vastly different anatomies.

Belinda held up the three-eyed glasses to her face and looked in the small mirror. Red, then green, then red again. Hadn't her mother said something about warm undertones looking best on her skin? She tried the green again. *Hm, no. Definitely no.* She picked up a heavy, chromatic yellow pair that looked almost gold in the bright lights of the souvenir shop. *Ooh, yes.*

'Doctor, look at these.' She turned around laughing, waving the three-eyed spectacles around. 'Now I've got twenty-twenty-*twenty* vision ...' But the Doctor was nowhere to be seen. Come to think of it, she couldn't remember when they had parted ways. She must have lost him in between the T-shirts and the bobble heads. 'Doctor?'

A hand settled on Belinda's shoulder from behind. Relief flooded through her as she turned. 'Doctor, thank goodness you're here ...' but it wasn't the Doctor standing behind her, brown-eyed and smiling. It was a mannequin, one from the front of the store. Belinda froze. The mannequins on the cruise were strange looking. On Earth, mannequins were mostly plain looking – all in the same colour, with no hair, or differentiating features, only vague impressions of faces, and long modelesque limbs. On the Moon Cruise, the mannequins were made with blonde hair in voluminous waves, blue eyes and a perfectly painted red mouth. They had all been dressed in a red and white pinstriped suit. Under the skirt, instead of legs, a large rolling sphere comprised the mannequin's lower half.

For just a moment, she felt her fight or flight activate, the thudding heart rate, the spike in adrenalin. Like she was prey, and the mannequin a predator, hunting by stealth.

Up close, the mannequin's skin was made of a smooth, nearly grainless wood, painted the same salmon-beige as the pencils labelled 'skin-colour' that had existed when Belinda was young. Her eyes were sapphire blue, the irises glassy and shiny. Two red pinpricks of light shone from within their depths. *Cameras,* Belinda realised.

The mannequin's mouth slid open, it's voice box chirping. 'Can I be of any assistance?'

Belinda stepped to the side, shaking the mannequin's hand off her shoulder. 'No, thank you.'

'Are any of these to your liking?'

'No, thank you,' Belinda smiled, shaking her head. 'I'm all right.' She looked around for the Doctor. She wouldn't be able to pay without him.

'The items can be charged to the room, if that is your preference. Please supply a room number.' The mannequin's docile gaze was feeling more and more like surveillance by the second.

'I – I don't –' Belinda gulped, getting a hold of herself. It was just a fancy robot, programmed to extract as many sales from each customer as possible. 'I don't need any assistance,' she said firmly. 'I'm just having a look. Thank you.'

The mannequin stood in front of her for a second longer, perfectly still. It was beyond disconcerting to be considered so intensely by a machine. Though, *machine* didn't quite feel like the right word. There was an intelligence in its eyes – dulled by its innocent appearance, but still there. Or maybe she was imagining things. Unsettled, Belinda was about to turn and walk away when the mannequin gave a soft whirr, its head tilting to one side. Its red mouth was fixed in a permanent smile.

'Enjoy your Moon Cruise experience.' It sounded like an order. 'And, whatever you do, be sure to have fun, fun, fun!'

Chapter Three

The Doctor peered at the sonic. It had started beeping a few minutes ago, just as they'd entered the souvenir shop. He'd let Belinda go on ahead, not wanting to alarm her after the great day they'd had. But the sonic kept beeping.

It was throwing out readings, seemingly at random. He turned it upside down, squinting at it. *What are you trying to warn me about?* Sometimes the sonic did this, almost like it was alive. They'd travelled together for so long, he felt like it was an extension of his brain, like another limb he could think and feel with . . .

And right now, he could feel that something was ever so slightly wrong.

His heart sank. He and Belinda had had such a nice day. He'd owed her that. No trouble, in and out. *Boring rocks*, that's what she'd asked for. Instead, they'd visited one of the most mysterious space cruises in history. Something nagged at him. There was more to the legend of the Moon Cruise than he could remember right now.

Something shadowy and sinister that had been exposed. He remembered seeing an interview with the leader of the cruise, an older woman with pale hair the colour of sage, her roots white. She'd been with her wife, a willowy woman with long dark hair in a braid over her shoulder. They'd led the crew through the disappearance, after the cruise had gone off course ... But why had that happened?

The Doctor shook his head. Maybe the sonic was just malfunctioning, causing him to see danger where there was none. Ever since he had found out that the planet 6-7-6-7 was Midnight, he had experienced a strange sense of time slipping away from him. A lack of control. A worried wondering whether he was forgetting things he shouldn't.

He looked up. At the entrance to the store, something was watching him. It looked like a mannequin, unmoving, and unblinking, its cartoonish blue eyes pinning him with their gaze.

Raising the sonic slowly, he pointed it right at the mannequin. The small device buzzed so hard it nearly dropped out of his hand. For just a moment, he looked down in shock.

When he looked back up, the mannequin was gone.

Belinda stood in the aisle, watching the mannequin retreat into the distance. It was surprisingly quick, racing down the aisle and out of sight. Cold aircon blew on the back of Belinda's neck, drying the sweat there. It was quiet in this aisle, the shelves a little dusty. Tinny music whined through the speakers, and the voices of other customers seemed muffled. She shook herself, walking back the way she had come. Towers of sunglasses surrounded her. *Where was the Doctor?* She had become so flustered during that interaction with the mannequin, it would have been nice to have had him there. She took another turn. Surely the Vindicator was nearly done. Maybe that's where he was – checking on it. Without looking where she was going, she took another turn, trying to convince herself that she recognised where she was. After fifteen minutes of frantic walking, she had to admit it. She was lost, and much deeper into the aisles than she had realised.

The stock on the shelves was older here, the plastic packaging covered in thick dust, the paper posters and postcards yellowing with age. She cast a look behind her, trying to remember the route, wondering if she should just turn back and find the Doctor. For a split second, the aisle seemed to glitch, before re-solidifying, the way behind her transformed into a dead-end. Belinda's breath caught. The lights above her were flickering. Perhaps the glitch was only a jumping shadow, caused by the malfunctioning light. Surely, a shelf could not have appeared out of nowhere to block her exit.

Voices ahead caught her attention. Frantic whispers, like two people arguing. She slowed down. The voices got closer. Belinda crouched, peeking through the shelves.

In the next aisle, a mannequin lay on the ground. Its painted blue eyes were dull, with no sign of the red camera light. Its lifeless limbs drooped to the sides, while its head was twisted at an odd angle. Two figures were crouched over it. One of them was very tall and muscular, a woman with long green hair tied in a ponytail. The other was smaller, but with a lean build, her hair scraped back in a dark braid. They both wore the blue jumpsuit uniform of crew members – the same as all the waiters in the restaurant had worn, the same as the staff who had massaged Belinda in the spa.

'Come on, V,' hissed the green-haired one. 'We only have a few minutes before they notice we've escaped and raise the alarm.'

Raise the alarm? What is she talking about? A dreadful sense of unease was creeping over her. She was so close she could make out their name tags. The green-haired one was named *Jax*. And the dark-haired one was *Vanessa*.

Vanessa knelt in front of the dead mannequin. She pressed an invisible panel on its front, exposing a jumble of wires. Without hesitation, she reached inside, pulling out a handful. Belinda flinched. It was like watching someone rip the intestines out of a corpse.

Vanessa looked at Jax. 'I'll go first. In case it doesn't

work, or it sets off an alarm, and they figure out that we are trying to escape. You'll still have time to run. Okay? Promise me you'll run?'

Reluctantly, Jax nodded. 'We'll meet on the upper decks. At the escape pods.'

'Exactly.' Without another word, Vanessa pressed the wires to the silver bracelet on her wrist. Jagged sparks of blue electricity shot out of the wire. She gave a sharp cry of pain. Then the bracelet snapped open with a sharp click and clattered to the floor. It flashed green once, and then the light died.

They both stared at it in disbelief. 'It worked,' Jax breathed. 'Oh my – it *worked*.'

'Quickly, Jax, come closer, I can't get you from there.' Vanessa drew the wire towards Jax's wrist. Jax set her jaw. 'Hold still, or you could die.' Vanessa plugged the wire into the bracelet. There was a click, and the bracelet fell off. But instead of flashing green, Jax's bracelet flashed red. And kept flashing red.

Jax's face drained of colour. 'Should I put it back on?'

'No!' Vanessa looked terrified. 'I – I don't know.'

'Run!' Jax yelled at her. 'You have to run. I—'

'I'm not going without you.'

'Run!' Jax shouted. 'I'll meet you at the escape pods. Just *go*. Or we'll both be killed.'

Vanessa got up and ran. She was sobbing. Her cries receded into the distance as she ran. Until Jax was alone.

In a fit of rage, Jax turned round, slamming her hand on the shelf that Belinda was hiding behind. Belinda gasped and jerked backwards.

It happened almost in slow motion. Belinda's foot caught on the bottom of the shelf. She was crouching, so she was already off kilter. Her arms shot out, trying to find something to stabilise herself with, and she knocked a stack of paperweights off the shelf. They clattered to the floor with a deafening crash.

Jax's eyes darted towards her. Their gazes locked.

Belinda froze.

Quick as lightning, Jax lunged. Her arms shot through the racks and grabbed Belinda by both wrists.

'Let me go!' Belinda yelled. 'Let me—'

Jax clamped the bracelet over her wrist. The vibrations shocked Belinda's skin, before they subsided, the red light turning off as it sensed her body heat and heartbeat. The bracelet went still.

Belinda and Jax looked down at it. Jax in relief, Belinda in horror. 'What have you done to me?' she whispered. Jax dropped her hands. Belinda scrambled backwards. They were still on opposite sides of the rack. Stock had been thrown everywhere during their struggle. For a moment, they just stared at each other.

'I'm sorry,' Jax choked out. 'I'm sorry.'

Then she took off in the same direction Vanessa had taken and Belinda was left alone.

*

She wandered the aisles for what felt like an eternity before she heard the sound of a crowd and ran towards it. She had to find the Doctor. Surely he would be able to use the sonic to get the bracelet off.

A whirring noise alerted her to the presence of a mannequin before one appeared in front of her, rolling at full speed. 'Crew member detected in an unauthorised zone,' it droned accusingly. 'Get back to work!'

'There's been a mistake. I don't—'

The mannequin's hand reached out, grabbing her shoulder. It steered her through the crowds, pushing her through a small door until they reached the tills. Except, this time, she was standing behind them as an employee, rather than in front of them as a customer. The mannequin passed its hand over her bracelet, scanning the thin loop of metal. Information of some kind must have been stored on it. 'Moderate infraction detected – too much break time taken. Punishment: six months' increased sentence time.'

The mannequin may as well have been speaking in code. Belinda gaped. 'Excuse me?'

But the mannequin just wheeled off.

'Hey, are you going to serve me or not!' a shrill voice echoed.

Belinda jumped. 'Oh!' She looked down at the screen. For a moment, alien script swam in front of her. Then the TARDIS's translation kicked in and she realised that, even a thousand light years from Earth and the baby beginnings of capitalism, working a till on concessions was the same as it had been in college. Even if the receipts were digital and there was no money but credits charged to a room number, the pattern was the same: scan, press, tap, receipt. She'd be fine. As long as no one asked her to refund something, or – heaven forbid – use a *gift card*. The Doctor would find her soon, she was sure of it. He'd take the bracelet off, and they'd get out of here. But it was best to lie low until then. *Scan, press, tap.*

'Would you like a receipt?'

'No.'

Belinda shrugged. 'Next customer, please!'

Scan, press, tap. 'Receipt? No, okay.' Eyes still glued to the screen. 'Next! How can I help you?'

A stern voice said. 'One lost companion, please.'

Belinda tore her eyes away from the screen. Reality seemed thin and under-saturated by comparison. Her eyes widened. The Doctor. She pointed accusingly at him. 'Where have you been?'

His eyes caught immediately on the bracelet. 'Oh, tell me that's not what I think it is?'

Belinda froze. At his tone, a pit of anxiety formed in her stomach. 'Tell you what's not what you think it is?'

He grabbed her wrist and narrowed his eyes. 'Titanium alloy on the outside.' He sniffed it. 'It's measuring your vitals, tracking your location, measuring and evaluating your KPIs.' He frowned and scanned it with the sonic. 'Apparently, you're not hitting targets on collecting customer data. It's feeding that data back to a central computer. In fact, *everything* is going back to that central computer...' The Doctor paused. 'Someone isn't pleased with your performance.' Almost on instinct, Belinda turned and looked towards the front of the store.

The blonde mannequin was staring at them, her beautiful face serene and calm, blue eyes unblinking, red lights flickering in their depths.

'Belinda,' the Doctor said quietly. 'You need to take that off, right now.'

'I can't,' she blurted out. 'I can't take it off.'

'Why not?'

'I just can't.' The words were a compulsion. They didn't come from her.

'Belinda, take it off.'

She reached her hand towards her wrist. Immediately, strange thoughts filled her mind. *Serve the Cruise. Be a good team member. Maximise the customer experience. Make Marilyn proud.* Her hand dropped away. 'I can't.' Her voice was a whisper. 'Doctor, help.'

The Doctor's eyes widened. 'Mind repulsion technology. It's advanced. Too advanced just to control your average retail worker. Something isn't right.' Behind him, a line of customers was growing, one by one.

Belinda's heart was thudding. 'Why can't I take it off?'

'It's the tech. The bracelet and your mind are like opposite poles on a set of magnets, repelling each other.

It's simple but effective. Why have a pair of manacles, or stun the wearer with an inhumane electric shock, when you can simply turn their own mind against them?' He reached out a hand. 'But these bracelets are coded to repel the wearer. So it shouldn't stop me.' His fingers closed around the bracelet. Almost immediately, the thoughts returned. But this time, they hurt, assaulting Belinda's psyche with terrible images of a past that wasn't hers. She saw Jax reaching for a loaf of bread, snatching it and stuffing it into her satchel, before walking off. She thought she had got away with it, when the shouts began. A damp cell, rodents scurrying over her legs, biting her –

'*Stop!*' Belinda snatched her hand away from the Doctor. But it was too late. The bracelet had grown tighter. Instead of lying flush against her wrist, it dug into the skin. It would have been impossible to slide even her pinkie finger between her forearm and the thin band.

'Who did this to you?'

'The worker,' Belinda blurted out. 'Jax. She killed a mannequin and escaped. But I—I don't know what she was escaping from.'

The Doctor's head whipped to the side. Belinda followed his eyeline to the door, where a tall young woman in a hooded jacket was pushing past the patrons, head down. She turned away from the mannequin as she left the store. But a piece of hair flittered in the breeze of the aircon. It was bright green.

'*Her.*' Belinda said. 'It was her.'

'I'll get after her.' The Doctor turned back to face her. 'Then I need to find the central computer and shut it down. Or at least break the connection between it and that bracelet. There's no other way to take it off without hurting you. Do what you can with the customers in the meantime, yeah? I'll be back as quick as I can.'

Before she could reply, he was gone. And the line behind him had only grown longer.

Chapter Four

The Doctor barrelled through the shop, eyes fixed on the green-haired girl who had given Belinda her bracelet. She moved fast through the crowds, single-minded and determined. Despite her pace, it wasn't hard to follow her; she stuck out like a sore thumb. The other cruise-goers were laid back and easy, wearing luxurious, impractical outfits. Silks and leather, feathers and pearls; all manner of rich fabrics draped over their bodies, jewels glimmering on necklaces and earrings. The patrons' skin glowed with good health and a lack of stress. Most walked slowly, laden with shopping bags, hands wrapped around iced drinks or hot fast food. By contrast, Jax was hunched over, glancing furtively at the shop fronts. Her shoes were worn-down trainers, so bland they might even have been standard issue. She looked more like a prisoner than someone with a retail job.

In front of him, Jax froze, ducking behind a pillar. The Doctor slowed his pace, not wanting to stop at the same time and give the game away. *What exactly is she hiding from?*

The answer rolled into view: a blonde mannequin, dressed in a red and white pinstriped skirt suit. Blonde eyelashes blinked up and down as its head turned from side to side on a slow, constant rotation. When its eyes passed over the Doctor, he saw a flash of red. Cameras.

Ahead of him, Jax was already on the move again, this time walking faster. She bumped into a family, and kept going without an apology. Bags scattered to the floor in her wake, and soon the Doctor was running to catch up.

'You're in a hurry,' he said, half out of breath as he jogged alongside her to keep up. 'Are you running away from something, or towards it?'

'Leave me alone,' she growled. 'Or I'll make you.'

They both swerved a booth selling candy to children. 'Why did you put that bracelet on Belinda?'

'You must have me mistaken, sir. I don't know a Belinda.'

'The one with the kind eyes, who is currently stuck behind your till doing your job. Look, I get it – work is a bore. But you signed up for this, you can't just swap yourself out for a stranger!'

Jax barged through another group of cruise-goers, as if he had never spoken. People were starting to stare.

'Wait!' the Doctor called.

Jax stopped short, so abruptly the Doctor nearly barrelled into her. She whirled round to face him. 'You listen to me, all right?' Her finger nearly jabbed him in the eye. 'This ship isn't what it seems. People get hurt here, including passengers who stick their nose in where it's not welcome.' She looked furious. 'I'm leaving. And I'm sorry about your friend, I am. But there's nothing you can say that will make me stay. I only have once chance to escape this place and I'm taking it, understand? If you don't leave me alone, I'll make you regret it—' Jax broke off, her eyes widening.

From behind the Doctor, a robotic voice declared, 'Disturbance reported on floor 83. Clean-up crew has been dispatched.'

Two mannequins were rolling down the concourse toward them. Shoppers parted for them, barely aware of their presence. A child laughed and pointed at them. They looked like fairground attractions, something you put a coin into so it would play a song.

But Jax's expression, which had been so tough moments before, crumpled into pure, unadulterated fear.

'Stop where you are,' the mannequins commanded in unison, 'or your sentence will be increased.'

Jax turned to the Doctor. 'Don't you *dare* follow me,' was all she said. She turned and sprinted down the corridor. The Doctor launched himself after her. He could not let her out of his sight. She was the only one who could help him find that central computer and take the bracelet off Belinda before she too was trapped here for ever.

Behind them, the mannequins picked up the pace. They were gaining, and fast. 'Refusal to follow a command. Sentence increased: one year.'

Jax swore over her shoulder at them. 'You think that scares me? You're wrong!'

'Insolence. Sentence increased: two years. Inappropriate speaking volume: three years. Profanity: four years.'

'What are they counting towards?' the Doctor puffed. 'What's the sentence?'

Jax groaned. 'I thought I told you not to follow me!' They swerved a family, crashing through a small café and slamming through the back entrance onto the parallel concourse. 'We can't let them get close—'

But it was too late. The mannequins whizzed forward, navigating the crowded café with ease and coming up on either side of them. Jax took a hard left, into another one of the shops. The Doctor followed. The mannequins swerved, skidding across the floor. One of them fell. Jax jumped over it and kept running, back down the main strip.

'Two targets escaping down corridor 17a, floor 83,' came the mannequin's report.

Ahead of them, they heard a loudspeaker crackling. 'Preparing to intercept.'

Something zapped past the Doctor. A flash of bright blue.

'They fire wires!' Jax shouted. 'Don't let them hit you . . .'

They rounded the corner to find another mannequin waiting for them. The intelligence of the ambush chilled the Doctor to the core, but he didn't have time to think about it. He saw a compartment open in the mannequin's chest. Bright blue electricity flashed and crackled.

'Intercepting now,' the mannequin said. The electricity shot out. It was a long wire, barbed on the end like a grappling hook, or an old-fashioned arrow, designed to catch onto clothes to deliver the current.

'Watch out—' the Doctor exclaimed. Before he could get another word out, Jax shoved him with her shoulder. He braced his arm, ready to crash through a wall or the glass front of a store, but instead the wall rippled around him, light and sound distorting for a moment.

He stumbled, falling into air, before crashing against the floor. He rolled once, twice, and then came to a stop. Jax followed swiftly after, tumbling to the ground. She jumped to her feet. 'Quickly!' She grabbed him, dragging him upwards and towards a tiny supply closet. 'Get in.'

They piled in, shutting the door just in time. A whirring sound whizzed past, the crackling of a robotic voice. 'No visual on the runaways. Will maintain the pursuit.'

The Doctor set his eyes to the gap between the doors. Two more mannequins whizzed past. After a few minutes, the corridor was clear. He and Jax stepped out, panting in relief.

'How did you do that?' he asked. 'You pushed me through a wall.'

'Some of the shops are holograms,' Jax panted. Her hands were on her knees, and she was red in the face. 'Ship isn't as big as it looks.'

'You saved my life. Thank you.'

She straightened up to face the Doctor, her expression serious. 'You're not a passenger, are you?'

'No.'

'What do you want from me? Why do you care so much about this Belinda?'

The Doctor felt that old knife, guilt, sliding between his ribs. 'She is my responsibility. She didn't ask to be here. I need to get her home. I promised.' A moment of silence. Jax's face stayed inscrutable. 'She's my friend.'

'Your friend?' Jax's blank expression was replaced with pure scorn. 'You think you're the only one who's ever had a friend? I have a friend, too. Vanessa.' She lifted her wrist. The Doctor saw a pale band of flesh above her thin, bony wrist, where the bracelet must have sat. Jax shook her wrist at him. 'It took me and her *seven years* to figure out how to get these bracelets off just *once* without alerting anyone.' Patches of red appeared high on her cheeks, tears wobbling in her eyes. 'And now Vanessa's gone. Her bracelet came off and deactivated, just like we planned. So I told her to run for it. It wasn't her fault that mine didn't turn off all the way. But now she could be dead for all I know. I just have to hope she escaped with her life.' The fight seemed to go out of her. 'Hope. That's all I have. All any of us have. Hope that one day, things might be different.'

The Doctor's mind was racing. Little things he had seen while on board the cruise, combined with strange incongruities in Jax's story. Details that didn't make any sense. 'Seven years? But the Moon Cruise only set sail six years ago.'

Jax wiped her tears away. 'Of course you wouldn't get it. You've got the look of the upper decks about you. Ignorant, arrogant, can't see what's right in front of your face.'

The Doctor looked upwards. 'I'm not a passenger. I've never been to the upper decks.'

'Me neither.' Jax's voice had an edge of steel to it now. 'But that changes today. I'm going up there. I'm going to find my best friend. Our plan was to meet by the escape pods in the upper decks. That's where she must have gone. It's the only way to get out of this prison.'

'Prison?' More puzzle pieces slotted into place in the Doctor's mind. The high-tech bracelets, the mannequins and their roving eyes. But he still couldn't quite see the whole picture. 'Your friend wanted to escape a job so badly she'd risk being adrift in space?'

'This isn't a job. This is a life sentence. Of course, they don't tell you that in the beginning. See, they call it a rehabilitation programme. But it's not.' She waved a hand around. Behind her, the hologram shimmered for a moment, and the Doctor thought he saw a figure in a pinstriped suit rolling steadily closer. 'The Moon Cruise is a cruise. For the passengers on the middle decks, and the stakeholders who live on the upper decks. But the entire operation is run by people like me. Prisoners, criminals.' Jax smiled, but it was a hollow smile, full of sadness and regret. 'Vermin. The scum of society.' She shook her head. 'At least, that's what they call us.'

'And you've been here all this time?'

Jax nodded. 'At first, after I was arrested, I was thrown into a mega-prison on some dusty asteroid a million miles from civilisation. I was a petty criminal; I was only supposed to do ten months, for crying out loud. But then they announced the Moon Programme, funded by Marilyn Moon.'

The Doctor nodded. 'The tech billionaire.'

'Trillionaire. She was giving us a second chance. Serve her and her customers for the rest of our sentences, and then leave with a good reference and an opportunity to start again. We were even supposed to get paid. I thought it was as good an idea as any. They shipped us out a few weeks later, and I've been here ever since. That was six years ago.' Jax rubbed her palm over the pale band of skin at her wrist. 'Every single person who works here is held against their will. Marilyn's determined to wring every last drop of life from us for her own gain, before she discards us and forgets we ever existed.' Her wry smile returned, sending chills down the Doctor's back. 'She's doomed us. Doomed us to the worst hell in the universe: serving the wealthiest people in the galaxy, on a cruise that never stops.'

The Doctor stared at her. 'And now your bracelet is on Belinda. They think she's you.'

Jax looked away. 'I did what I had to do.'

'You've condemned an innocent person.'

'*I* was an innocent person!' Jax yelled. 'Trying to feed my family. That's all it was. I stole some food. And now I don't know if my family are okay. I don't even know if they're alive.' She glared at him. 'I'm sorry about your friend! I am. But Vanessa's my friend and I have to get to her.' Jax's glare turned darker. 'And if anything's happened to her I'll make all the upper decks pay.'

The Doctor knew deep down that despite Jax's prickly exterior, and despite the situation she had put Belinda in, she wasn't a bad person. If she was, she wouldn't have saved him from the mannequins. In fact, she probably would have pushed him in front of them to buy herself more time. She was just scared and lost, adrift in a galaxy that had chewed her up and locked her in chains without an explanation. It wasn't only unfair, it was despicable.

But Belinda shouldn't be made to pay the price.

The Doctor spoke quietly. 'I think there's a future where you and I both walk out of here free, with our friends safe by our sides. But you'll have to trust me, Jax. Can you?'

Chapter Five

'Serve with a smile!'

Belinda's hands on the screen were sweaty; her heart was palpitating. It felt like hours since the Doctor had run off, and processing the transactions wasn't as easy as it seemed. She kept making mistakes: charging for things twice, billing the wrong room. The mannequin manager had become a permanent fixture over her shoulder, reminding her to do inane things like serve with a smile, and –

'Remember to make Marilyn proud, Jax.'

'I'm not Jax!' Belinda blurted out in frustration. She half expected lasers to shoot from the mannequin's eyes and incinerate her, but she had realised fairly quickly that whatever form of artificial intelligence lay behind those limpid blue eyes was very, very basic.

'Teamwork makes the Moon Cruise dream work!' the mannequin intoned chirpily.

Where was the Doctor?

'Hey!' Another angry customer. A pair of glasses

clattered onto the counter. 'I want these in green. Where's the green?'

Despite the customer's abrasive tone, relief flared to life in Belinda's chest. She tapped the request into the till, confirming her suspicions. REPLENISHMENT NEEDED. They didn't have green sunglasses in that shape or style on the shop floor. She turned to the mannequin. 'I'm going to the storeroom.' She had spotted it an hour or so ago – a door at the far end of the shop. The shop floor was far bigger than she'd thought when she first entered it, which felt like a lifetime ago now. She supposed that was the trick of it – customers thought they were only popping into a small boutique for a souvenir, but before long found themselves lost among the maze-like aisles, getting subtly manipulated into spending more money by the overzealous mannequins. The only glimpses she had got of other employees had been as they walked down the aisle to the storeroom, disappearing into it and returning a few minutes later with boxes of stock. She must have seen four or five other employees, all in jumpsuits. Each time, she had tried to catch their eyes, to no avail. They didn't want to look at her – or be seen looking at her – instead of doing their jobs. It was hopeless. With no Doctor, she had no idea how she was going to get out of here.

Without waiting for the mannequin to respond, she left the tills, half-walking half-running to the double doors. She barrelled through them, immediately grateful to feel a cool soothing breeze on her hot sweaty face. For a moment, she stood in stillness with her eyes closed. It felt like heaven.

When she opened her eyes, reality hit. The storeroom was cramped, dank and cold. As her eyes adjusted to the dark, she saw boxes littering the floor, glasses and postcards spilling out onto the ground. There was mould growing on a stack of T-shirts. Pipes overhead dripped water at the bends, and a crusted layer of stale water and dust had settled over the walls and floor. It was clear the mannequins didn't police this area as much as they did the shop. *Only concerned with outward appearances,* she thought bitterly.

Her legs were trembling. It felt like years since the Doctor had run off after Jax. She felt tears well in her eyes. This was ridiculous. She needed to get out of here. She'd almost made a run for it several times, but each time the same thing stopped her. The mannequin. Despite its stupid stock phrases, its strange blue gaze felt intelligent, the whirring noise of its inner mechanisms sounded like a warning. And she could not forget the terror on Jax's face as she'd watched it approach over Belinda's shoulder. What were they capable of?

With a yell, she slammed the bracelet against the wall. Nothing happened. If anything, she began to feel strangely nauseous – the bracelet's mind-influencing abilities at play, no doubt. Wiping her eyes, she looked around the storeroom for an exit.

There.

A door marked with the universal symbol of a flame, and a running biped. Fire exit. There was only one thing for it. She would go through it and run until she found the TARDIS where they'd left it in the access corridors. Then she'd lock herself inside until the Doctor came back. Simple. What could go wrong?

Resolved, she ran over to it, pushing on it firmly with both hands.

Nothing. Not the slightest bit of give. 'Let me out!' she yelled, hammering on it. 'I don't belong here!'

Something on the doors caught her sleeve, almost tearing it. Gently, she unhooked it, peering at the doors. There was an old framed poster stuck to the left door, hidden away under the thick layer of dust and grime that had accumulated all over the storeroom. Using her sleeve, Belinda wiped away some of the grime.

Slowly, a woman's face was revealed. A pointed chin, a red mouth curved in a smile, and finally, big blue eyes, beaming out from under a blonde updo, curled tendrils framing her face. A vintage-looking pinstriped skirt suit in red and white hugged her petite frame. She looked like an old Hollywood starlet. Belinda scrubbed harder, using her whole sleeve. Section by section the poster was revealed in its entirety, including a gold plaque that sat directly underneath it, inscribed with the woman's name.

'Pictured here is the successful businesswoman and lauded philanthropist Marilyn Moon,' Belinda read, her voice a whisper. 'Founder of Intragalactic Cruises Limited, and Director of the Moon Cruise Convicts' Rehabilitation Programme, Marilyn has changed the face of commercial space travel, bringing it into the twenty-sixth century.'

It was the same woman who had been interviewed on the TV in the spa. Her face was all over the cruise. And while Belinda had been working, she'd seen the woman featured in several of the infomercials that played for ten minutes at a time between the scheduled programming. She sold everything from motion sickness tablets to movies that she'd starred in, available to watch on the streaming service she had created for the cruise. She promoted her own clothing line, and encouraged passengers to upgrade their rooms or suites to more expensive options.

Behind her, the door swung open. Belinda's heart leapt into her mouth. The blonde mannequin stood in the doorway, its head tilted to the side. Belinda stared at it, her heart sinking. It was so obvious now. *The mannequins are made in Marilyn's image.*

'Don't disappoint me, Jax,' the mannequin intoned. 'I gave you a second chance, remember?'

It was a totally different speech pattern to the one the mannequin used in front of customers. The chirpiness was gone, replaced instead by something more sinister.

Belinda snatched an overflowing box of glasses off the shelf of stock, edged past the mannequin and left.

*

'Can you trust me, Jax?' The Doctor kept his voice soft. She looked uncertain, her eyes darting between him and the corridor behind. He waved the sonic to hook her attention. 'This can get us there. I've locked it on to the central computer – the one that controls the bracelets. It's my only chance of freeing Belinda. I'll do whatever it takes to get that thing off her. And if that means teaming up with you, I'm all for it.'

Jax looked sceptically at the sonic. 'That thing can get us to the upper decks? Even the passengers on the upper deck can't leave. And why would they want to? Apparently, it's paradise.'

'Think about it. If they're always offering people upgrades, trying to get them to pay more to go up to the highest levels, there's got to be a way for regular passengers to access the upper decks. And what about staff? They need people to work there.'

Jax nodded. 'I heard from a friend: there's a staircase. Takes hours to climb, but it's been forgotten about because the mannequins can't use stairs. That's where Vanessa went.' Jax looked up, towards the ceiling. 'I hope she made it.'

'So we're agreed? I'll come with you, to the upper decks. Chaperone you, so no one questions your presence. We can use this,' he waved the sonic, 'to reveal shortcuts, and hiding places. Nooks and crannies. Love a nook and cranny.'

Jax raised an eyebrow. 'Why would you do that for me?'

He shrugged. 'You said Marilyn Moon was a bully. And I don't like bullies.'

Chapter Six

Back on the shop floor, an identical copy of the Marilyn mannequin was waiting for Belinda behind the till. She stopped short.

'Your shift is over,' it said. 'I will escort you to the meeting point.'

Relief flooded through Belinda's system. *Finally.* She was going to find the Doctor and, hopefully, Jax so she could wring her neck. This had been the most bizarre, stressful and terrifying day in a while, which was saying something when you travelled with someone like the Doctor.

'Now,' the mannequin demanded.

Hesitantly, Belinda nodded, following the mannequin as it weaved through customers and exited the store. They walked a short way down the main strip of the mall, before the mannequin stopped in front of a blank section of wall between two storefronts. Its eyes glowed red. For a moment, nothing happened. Belinda began to edge away from the mannequin, wondering if she should just make a run for it. Then the wall disappeared. It blinked out of existence between one breath and the next. A hologram.

A line of workers stood in the dark, damp corridor beyond the wall. Their shoulders were slumped, their heads bent. They were all holding hands – no, they were all *linked* via their bracelets.

The mannequin's wires emerged from a hidden panel, glowing with a faint blue light. Belinda's arm snapped upward, the bracelet dragging her wrist into the air. All around her, the other prisoner's bracelets had done the same. With a vibrating hum, all the bracelets flashed.

Belinda felt her entire body go rigid—she was locked in place, chained by the bracelet's energy into this line of prisoners, unable to move except to walk forward.

'Stop,' Belinda said. 'Wait, I thought—'

'What?' someone grumbled. 'That you were going home? That's a good one. You must be new here.'

'Prisoners must not communicate with one another.'

Prisoners? Belinda's eyes widened.

The man directly in front of her peered at her strangely. 'Isn't this Jax's shift? Who are you? Why aren't you wearing a uniform?'

'Because *I don't work here*! Jax forced the bracelet on me after she tried to take it off and I didn't work—'

The man jolted back. 'Jax's gone?' A wide-eyed expression came over his face. 'So she did it,' he murmured. 'She actually did it. Her and Vanessa. I never thought . . .' He shook his head at Belinda. 'You can't hold it against her, what she did. It's rough for you, but you'd have done the same thing for a chance at your old life back.'

'What are you talking about?'

But before the man could reply, the mannequin turned to face them. A panel opened in its mid-section, pinstripes parting to reveal a dark black square. Belinda saw a glowing length of wire shoot out and connect with the man's torso. Electricity crackled. His entire body went rigid, juddering violently. He gurgled unintelligibly, before slumping forward, held upright by the person in front.

Automatically, Belinda started forward to help him. *'Did you just electrocute him?'* The words had scarcely left her mouth before the wire flickered again, swift as a snake's tongue. She twisted her body, desperately trying to move away. But the end of it caught her on the elbow, tiny hooks embedding themselves in the cotton of her jacket. The effect was instantaneous. White light scattered across her vision, the entire corridor disappearing in a flash of blue-white. Every cell felt like it had been set on fire, her blood was lava, her eyes felt like hot grapes crushed underneath a boot-heel. Her knees collided with something cold and hard and, at the same time, her head hit something soft. She opened her eyes and saw the back of the jumpsuit of the man in front of her. She had fallen forward; the only thing keeping her upright was the bracelet, and the line of workers.

'Somebody get her up,' whispered a harsh and angry voice, 'or we'll all be punished.'

The last thing Belinda felt before darkness washed over

her like a wave were rough hands under her armpits, hauling her back into a standing position.

'We're lost, aren't we?' Jax said. 'You told me you knew how to get to the upper decks.'

'I *do*.' The Doctor shook the sonic. 'This has been going haywire since we got here.' He gestured toward the ceiling. 'We need to get out of . . . whatever this place is. I think the trees are blocking the signal.'

They were walking through a jungle. It was fake, of course, just like everything on board the ship, but so beautifully crafted that the Doctor closed his eyes to breathe in the chlorophyll and rainwater-on-earth scent, replicated almost perfectly. Tiny, jewel-like birds darted in and out of the trees in flashes of colour, whistling a disjointed song. An iguana ambled across the path in front of them, and the bright eyes of monkeys blinked down from the branches above.

The sonic recalibrated, leading them down the path. They kept their heads low, passing lots of couples out for a romantic evening stroll in the verdant green of the forest. Luckily, they all had eyes for no one but each other, and Jax and the Doctor passed without drawing much attention.

'No one knows where the mannequins come from,' Jax explained under her breath as they crept through pathways, sticking to the side of the path, where the dappled shadows that filtered through the faraway canopy shifted and rippled, hiding their faces. 'There seem to be more and more every year. And they're getting more vicious too. They used to be more like security guards, keeping us in line by increasing our sentences at the slightest provocation. But then people started to realise the sentences were meaningless. There were people who were only supposed to serve a year on the ship, and then get a shuttle back home. But the shuttles never arrived. The world forgot about us, and Marilyn just kept adding more time to our sentences. She's found a way to keep us here for ever, and any attempt we make to escape only prolongs our time here.'

They were almost at the end of the jungle path when Jax stopped short in front of the Doctor, so quickly he nearly bumped into her. A little boy in a sailor's costume was standing in their path, holding a huge fairground lollipop in one hand. Red and blue candy was smeared all over his face. 'Why is your hair green?' he asked Jax.

Jax blinked. 'Er . . .'

'It just grows that like,' the Doctor replied with a smile. 'Run along now.'

'I've seen you before,' the boy said. Then his eyes widened. 'You're on all the TVs!'

'Shh!' The Doctor knelt down in front of the boy. 'No need to tell the world.' He pointed at Jax. 'She's a celebrity. A special guest of Marilyn Moon. She's here on secret business, so you can't tell a soul.'

'No, she's not.' The little boy was backing away. His lollipop dropped to the ground, forgotten. 'She's a criminal! My mummy said if we saw her, we were supposed to shout, really, really, loudly.' He took a huge breath.

The Doctor looked at Jax. 'Run!

'HELP!' the boy bellowed. 'HELP ME!'

Immediately, they heard a whirring sound. Red and white flashed through the trees.

'Mannequin!' Jax yelled. 'Doctor, how do we get out of here?'

The Doctor was following the sounds of the sonic. 'This way.'

They sprinted down the gravel path. Couples were pushed apart as they barrelled through them.

The mannequin cut through the trees, electric wires crackling in each of its hands. 'Resisting pursuit: five years. Breaking contract: six years. Not serving the required notice period: seven years.'

'We need to go through the trees!' the Doctor yelled. 'There's a river – across it, there's another exit. If we cross the water, maybe we can lose them.'

Jax nodded, and they plunged into the trees. Tiny branches whipped across the Doctor's face, and vines seemed to rear up and snarl, curling over his legs and feet, trying to trip him. He could hear the sound of running water. Before long they arrived on the banks of a small river. It looked almost too wide to jump across.

Jax must have had the same thought. She started rolling up her trouser legs, preparing to jump in and wade.

'Wait!' The Doctor pointed to a sign.

Preserved in this recreation of the fabled Amazon River are a rare and ancient species of fish: Pygocentrus nattereri, more commonly known as the red-bellied piranha. These fish, while not originally aggressive, have acquired an unexplained taste for living flesh.

Jax leapt back. 'We can't go round it. What do we do?'

'We'll have to jump. I'll go first.' Without stopping to think, the Doctor took several paces back before running and launching himself over the side of the river. He flailed his arms, hoping to propel himself further. The bank rushed up to meet him. SMACK. Slamming into the dirt, he rolled to the side just in time to see Jax run and jump. At the last moment, her foot caught on a root. She tipped forward, slapping onto the surface of the piranha-infested waters.

The Doctor crawled forward, holding out an arm. Desperately Jax half-ran, half-swam through the murky river. Sliver shapes flitted close to the surface. 'Take my hand.' But she was too far away.

Suddenly, a rope flew over the Doctor's head. It was knotted at regular intervals, perfect for someone to hold on to. Jax grabbed it, hauling herself towards the bank, just as the river erupted in frenzied snapping. The water churned white as Jax flopped onto the bank, out of reach.

The Doctor heard a whirr. The mannequin whizzed out of cover by the trees, stopping just short of the river. 'Seeking alternative route,' it stated, then headed back the way it had come.

'You need to get out of here,' said a voice. The Doctor and Jax turned round. A middle-aged woman held the rope. She wore a navy jumpsuit and a silver bracelet. Another prisoner.

'Eleanor. Thank you,' Jax said. 'How can I ever repay you—'

'Escape. That's how.' Eleanor gave Jax a gentle push. 'The door is that way. Don't get caught. Oh, and take this.' She handed Jax a broom with a long metal handle, and a pair of rubber gloves. 'Put these on. Now, quickly.' Jax obeyed. Eleanor smiled grimly. 'They're not as cleverly made as Marilyn thinks they are. Metal conducts electricity, the rubber gloves will protect you. Now go.'

Jax paused for a moment, clutching the broom to her chest as if it were the most precious thing in the galaxy. She looked at Eleanor with wide eyes – eyes that glimmered with unshed tears.

The Doctor watched them exchange a look of camaraderie. With an uncharacteristically tender look on her face, Jax reached out, touching Eleanor's upper arm in acknowledgement of her gratitude and their shared struggle as prisoners of Marilyn Moon's cruelty. It was likely that Eleanor would be punished for helping Jax escape, the Doctor realised. But she had done it anyway.

'Go!' Eleanor hissed. 'Or it will all have been for nothing!'

Without another word, Jax and the Doctor ran past her to the tunnels that led back into the ship.

Chapter Seven

The Doctor and Jax almost made it.

Just as the doors had closed behind them, Eleanor disappearing from view, the mannequin from the forest burst into the corridor. Leaves were caught in the wooden curls of its blonde hair, and the electric wires were bright with power.

'*Stop!*' it commanded. 'Stop now, and Marilyn will be merciful.'

'No,' Jax yelled. She kept running. The Doctor followed.

The mannequin released the electric wires. They snapped forward, crackling intensely, each barb glowing with the deadly current. But Jax was prepared. She held the broom out in both hands, crossed over her mid-section like a battle staff. The wires slammed into it, wrapping around the pole. Jax held firm, even as she was tugged forward. A blinding flash of white light lit up the corridor. Jax screamed and dropped the broom. But the damage was done.

When the light faded, the mannequin was lying on its back.

'Eleanor was right,' Jax breathed. 'The broom handle made a sort of circuit out of the wires. The charge was reversed.'

A dark plume of acrid smoke curled from a joint in the mannequin's neck, which was snapped at a strange angle like a broken hinge. The whirring sphere it rolled around on was still. Light reflected off the glass panes of its eyes, which were open and staring blindly upward.

As the Doctor got closer, he saw that the red lights were still on, flickering in and out like faulty torch beams. There was still something left alive inside the mannequin – the AI, or whatever it was that powered the strange doll-like sentries, hadn't been totally annihilated by the reversed blast.

Jax walked towards the mannequin, her hands clenched into fists.

'Careful,' he warned her, but she didn't seem to hear him. He peered closer. The red lights were fading, little by little. Clearly, the mannequin was reluctant to let go of the strange life it had led on board the cruise.

Jax stepped closer to it. For a moment, she didn't say anything; she just circled it, eyes searching its face for something. Fear and disgust warred on her face, until disgust won.

'How does it feel?' she asked quietly. 'To be helpless?'

The mannequin gurgled something unintelligible.

Jax laughed bitterly. 'Are you wondering where your overlord Marilyn is now? Or have you realised there's no one coming to save you? You're all alone. Expendable. A product they'll use for their own gain, and then swap out when it's faulty, or broken, or no good.'

Another gurgle, even quieter than the last.

'Careful,' the Doctor murmured again.

She ignored him. 'I almost feel sorry for you. A mindless prison guard, created with only one purpose: make others' lives a misery.'

The mannequin gurgled again. 'Jax...'

Jax sneered. 'Oh, I'm not falling for that. You call us by our names after scanning our bracelets, so that we feel like you know us, and we become less likely to attack you and try to escape.' She shook her head. 'I'm not that stupid.'

The Doctor's gaze darted to Jax's bare wrist – the pale line of skin. 'Jax,' he warned. 'You're not wearing your bracelet.'

'Jax...' the mannequin gurgled. 'Help me...'

Jax froze. She stared at her own wrist, as if in disbelief. Then she looked back at the mannequin. 'How did you identify me? Have they upgraded the tech? You can scan our faces now, or something? I'm surprised Miss Moon shelled out the cash.'

The Doctor shook his head, remembering the sonic's diagnosis when he'd scanned the mannequin-bot over his shoulder earlier. 'The bots are cheap. Mass-produced sentries. It's cheaper for Marilyn to keep replacing them with new versions of the same model than repair or upgrade the units she already has.'

'Why should she care about what's cheap? She has more money than anyone.'

'Jax . . .' The mannequin's voice was garbled and wet.

'Oh, for goodness' sake!' In a fit of anger, Jax kicked the mannequin. The toe of her boot caught the edge of the broken neck, and the mannequin's head flopped to the side. The impact sent the front panel of the face sliding off, clattering against the floor so loudly that echoes raced around the corridor.

Crash, crash. crash.

The Doctor expected to see a tangle of wires, perhaps a simple computer, or an incredibly basic AI. He wasn't prepared to see a face.

'Oh!' Jax's hands flew up to her mouth. '*Oh no.*'

Inside the mannequin's round head, a man's face lolled to one side. His pale skin was grey, almost translucent. For a moment, the Doctor wondered if it was a very realistic model, made out of silicon in a strange imitation of skin. A tracery of blue veins branched all over the man's gaunt cheeks, stretching past chapped, blue lips and half-closed eyes that were still emitting a faint red light. But then his mouth opened again. 'Jax, help me.' His voice was little more than a whisper now. The helplessness in his tone pierced the Doctor straight to the core. What kind of monster was responsible for this horror?

Jax fell to her knees. Her face, which had shown nothing but anger and derision, with occasional hints of fear, since the Doctor had first chased her down outside the glasses shop, was now filled with grief. 'No, no, no,' she whispered. 'Martin, who did this to you?'

Martin. She hadn't mentioned a Martin, but the Doctor would have wagered all the money in the casino that they had known each other well, once.

Jax's hand came up and touched Martin's cheek. His face turned, mechanisms whirring. It was awful, what they'd done to him. The rest of his body had been cut away, to fit his face and brain inside the mannequin. A tangle of nerve endings were clustered under the remains of his spinal cord, fused with wires so that his brain could still control the movements of the mannequin. The Doctor felt a very old anger rise in him then, an anger he thought he had shaken off, once and for all. But emotions were just like any other energy; they could not be destroyed, only changed or transformed into something else. That was why he didn't like to stay still in one place for too long: every feeling turned back into anger eventually.

Jax was sobbing quietly; Martin's eyes were almost closed now. He mumbled something. Jax put her ear closer to his face, nodding. Her hand never left his cheek. After a few moments, she sat back up. 'Thank you, Martin.' Jax's whisper was choked off with tears. She knelt for a few moments more, before wiping her eyes, rising and turning to face the Doctor. 'He's gone,' she said quietly.

The Doctor was silent for a moment. 'Who was he to you? Martin?'

At the sound of Martin's name, she closed her eyes. 'No one, really. Not in the grand scheme of things.' She sighed. 'We worked the bar at the casino on level fifty-three together, our first two years here. We used to lock ourselves inside the fridge freezers until our lips were blue, because the mannequins couldn't come inside – the low temperatures messed with their programming. We'd just talk, and joke around. But ... Martin used to give out free chips to nice patrons. I always pretended not to notice – and why should it have mattered to me? That was back when we thought we'd be let go after our sentences were served. One day, Martin was taken back to the barracks early. The higher-ups had found discrepancies in the casino's books. They took him away for questioning. After that, I never saw him again.' She looked back at the lifeless body on the ground. 'All these years, he's been patrolling the cruise, trapped inside a cage. I thought he was dead.'

'In a way, he was,' the Doctor said. 'That was not a life. Martin stopped existing the moment they destroyed his body to make that *thing*.'

Jax put her head in her hands. In a whisper, she confessed, 'All I can think about is Vanessa.' Her voice was choked. 'What if she's waiting somewhere for me, and we don't get to her in time? What if I'm too late, and they drag her off to be recycled into a robot?'

'No,' the Doctor said abruptly. 'That is absolutely not happening.'

'You can't be sure.' Jax rubbed a hand over her face. 'Sorry. Today has taken its toll on me. I didn't think I'd be doing this alone. Vanessa was supposed to be here.' She paused for a moment, composing herself. 'We can still get to the staircase from here. From there, the route to the escape pods in the upper decks is simple. Evacuation protocol states that in the event of an emergency, everyone on the upper decks must congregate in the auditorium. There's a tunnel underneath the stage that leads straight to the escape pods.' She pointed down the corridor. 'The access lift down there leads to the staircase, which opens up in the abandoned guards' barracks on the upper decks. They're empty now, so we can use them as our entry point.'

'Why were they abandoned?'

'No one knows for certain, but if I had to guess ... Before the mannequins, there used to be security guards. Real ones, living breathing people, employed to keep us in check. They slowly started disappearing at around the same time that the mannequins started to increase in number. I'd bet that they were taken to be the first set of mannequins. The prototype. And Marilyn is nothing if not greedy, so I'm certain that when she saw how well they worked ...' Jax trailed off, disgust clear on her face.

'She knew she could do the same to the prisoners,' the Doctor concluded.

Jax nodded. 'That's why I have to get out of here. There's no limit to the horrors she is willing to inflict on us just to make her profits bigger. None of us are people to her. We're all just a means to an end.' She looked back at Martin, his pale face, mostly in shadow, staring out from inside the stiff body of the mannequin.

The Doctor wondered if she saw Vanessa's fate. He surprised himself by saying softly, 'We'll find her, Jax.'

'How can you be sure, Doctor?'

'We're closer than we've ever been. But we don't stand a chance if we just sit around talking about it.' He pointed to the end of the corridor. 'And right now, our best chance of finding her is through that door. On the upper decks.' He offered her his hand. For a moment, he didn't think she'd take it. Then her fingers closed around his. 'Come on. Let's go and find Vanessa.'

And the central computer, he thought, as they made their way towards the door. *So that I can save Belinda, and get her home.*

Chapter Eight

Belinda and the other prisoners were marched through the musty corridors in total silence. She stared at her feet, trying to memorise each turn she made, reversing their long journey in her mind so that, when she finally escaped, she could retrace her steps. But the corridors all looked the same – blank stretches of damp grey concrete, differentiated only by patches of black mould and scummy puddles created by leaking pipes. In the more humid corridors, the pale caps of white mushrooms sprang up out of the cracks between the floor and the wall, their slender stems clustered in thick patches of fungal growth.

With a shudder, Belinda couldn't help but think of her time on Stenlar, where the local fungus had infected the inhabitants. *I'll never eat a mushroom again.*

Rights became lefts, lefts became rights. Usually, she had a fantastic memory – memorising medical terms had been a breeze when training to become a nurse – but her mind felt groggy from the electric shock, and the directions slipped away like water through a sieve.

The mannequin in front of them was silent, the only noises the whirr and click of its internal mechanisms and the shuffling feet of the other prisoners. At times the hologram walls flickered, allowing the prisoners to see the luxury façade of shops, boutiques, cinemas and bars. It felt like a glimpse into another world. One that was totally inaccessible to her.

They turned another corner. Belinda was so close to the wall that, when it vanished for just a moment, she stood shoulder to shoulder with the patrons of the cruise as they laughed and teased one another, eating ice cream and pressing their faces to the large, round windows that looked out onto the vastness of space. Their eyes passed right over her and the line of prisoners she was joined to. She was just turning back when she saw him.

The Doctor. He was running through what looked like a forest, hand thrust over his shoulder, sonic shining in his hand. And next to him – Jax! For a moment Belinda's heart swelled with hope. He'd found Jax, he was going to tackle her and drag her back to Belinda, use some clever words to convince her to take the bracelet back, and then Belinda would be free to get home from this stupid adventure that she had never asked for.

Then the Doctor grabbed Jax's hand. They ran past Belinda, unable to see or hear her.

'Doctor!' she screamed. '*Doctor, I'm right here!*'

Someone's hands came up from behind her, muffling her cries. 'Shut up! Or we'll all get our sentences increased – ow!'

She bit the hand, tearing her face out of its grip. 'Doctor, I'm here. *Can't you hear me?*'

He couldn't. The wall flickered back into being. Solid, and so real looking. She had half a mind to reach out and touch it, to see if the cold hard slab of stone would let her through if she pushed hard enough, but the mannequin appeared behind her.

'Ten years increased sentence for group 67A. And twenty years for Prisoner Jax.' Frustrated groans broke out. The mannequin whirred and then a high-pitched *ding* sounded. Belinda's bracelet buzzed, and she heard the answering vibrations of the other bracelets buzzing, too. 'System updated.' The mannequin chirped. 'Proceed to the bunkers.'

They descended through the levels, eventually reaching a large lift which took them down even further into the belly of the ship. When the lift doors opened, Belinda found herself in near-darkness. Faint red hazard lights were the only things that lit the way. As they walked, Belinda realised they were in an enormous underground barracks. She could hear the sounds of people sleeping, murmuring to themselves and to each other. An echoing snore made her jump. But she couldn't see any beds. Or people for that matter. They came to a halt.

'Prisoners are relieved from their duties.' The mannequin's wires flickered. The energy field dissipated, the bracelets flashing. The strange forcefield that had locked them in place, preventing them from escaping the chain of prisoners, was gone. 'Moon Cruise Incorporated thanks you for your service. Goodnight.' The mannequin turned and whirred away.

Belinda rubbed her wrists, grateful to be in control of her own body once again. Everyone just stood still, as if they were waiting for something.

Without warning, the floor jolted. A slow grinding noise started, like metal against rock. Belinda looked down. Her bracelet was glowing blue, matching with a glowing blue circle that had activated beneath her feet. The floor was *moving*, the circular piece of stone she stood on descending.

Within moments, she was knee deep, and the floor was rising quicker and quicker, swallowing her. 'What's going on?' she whispered frantically.

'Personal oubliettes,' a voice whispered to her left. *Oubliette?* That sounded like a medieval torture device. She turned in time to see the man who had been in line behind her. The one who had asked her where Jax was. For a moment, she wasn't certain if he had actually spoken, or not. His eyes darted around fearfully, his teeth worrying his bottom lip, anxiety clear in every facet of his expression. They were chest-deep in the chambers beneath the floor before he looked back at her and spoke again. 'The sleeping chambers are oubliettes. Small chambers, roughly the same size and shape as the prisoner assigned to them. There's enough room to turn over, but not enough to allow excessive movement.'

'Why aren't we allowed to move?'

His voice went even quieter. 'Because the bracelets power off at night, too. The servers that control them use huge amounts of energy. The ship can't generate enough to keep all of them on all the time – so they can only track people on shift. In about an hour, the light will turn red, that's how you know you've got ten minutes of light left. Ten minutes until the bracelet powers off.' His eyes darted to the doorway. They could barely see it now. 'Remember,' he whispered. 'Jax was much taller than you . . .'

Then his face was gone, and the chamber was closing over her head, sealing her in darkness.

It was warmer than she'd thought, inside the oubliette. The walls were made of a matte black metal, and there was bedding inside it, folded up in a neat heap at the bottom. Belinda frowned. Surely they didn't expect them to sleep standing up? Not that it mattered. She wasn't going to sleep; she was going to escape. She couldn't wait around any longer. The Doctor wasn't coming to save her, so she would have to save herself.

She felt around the walls. Her finger brushed an indentation in the wall. A button. She pressed it, and a warning beep sounded. She half-expected the entire chamber to self-destruct. But instead, a small, shallow drawer popped out of the side of the chamber, near to her face. For Jax, it would have been about chest level. Inside was a loop of braided cloth. Red and purple, entwined, the coarse fabric woven with care until it was tight as rope. There was a small charm in the centre of it – a tiny silver 'V'. It was a necklace, she realised, and felt her heart soften.

'V for... what? Or who?' She brushed her thumb over the charm. *Vanessa*, she realised. It must have belonged to Vanessa. It looked polished, and well taken care of. Clearly, it was a dear possession of Jax's. She had left it behind in her haste to escape this nightmare. For the first time, Belinda wondered how long Jax had been held prisoner here. Sleeping in an oubliette so small the most she could do was roll over in her sleep, or pull a blanket up to her chin.

A snippet of speech came back to her. The prisoner who had given her the clue about the bracelet. When he'd noticed who she was, he'd said, *You can't hold it against her, what she did... You'd have done the same thing, for a chance at your old life back.*

A chance at your old life back. It was funny, wasn't it? The way the universe consistently conspired to show you the irony in your own actions. She'd said as much to the Doctor, just before they'd opened the TARDIS doors and stepped on board the cruise. *I'd like my old life back!* And now she had become a pawn in someone else's plan to get back to *their* old life, lowering the odds of Belinda getting home by several orders of magnitude.

On an impulse, she grabbed the woven necklace and slipped it over her head, so that the V rested in the hollow of her throat, cool and comforting against her skin. If she found the Doctor again, and he was still with Jax – if whatever was chasing them hadn't caught up to them and taken them to some high-tech bunker-dungeon – she'd be able to give the woven cord with its charm back to her. Restlessly, she checked her bracelet. It was still glowing with a faint blue light. No sign of any red yet.

With a sigh, she pressed the button again and the drawer disappeared. Beside it was a switch. She flipped it absent-mindedly.

The chamber she was in began to tilt. 'No, no, no –' she slid sideways, hands unable to find anything to hold on to. Eventually, the chamber lay horizontal, and she was forced to lie down. The ceiling was inches from her face. An intense sense of claustrophobia gripped her. Scrabbling at the wall, she stabbed the button again, breathing out in relief as the chamber tilted back upwards. When it was fully upright, she leaned against the wall, grateful that she at least had the space to crouch down. *Jax was much taller than you,* the other prisoner had said. *When the light goes red, you've got ten minutes until the bracelet powers off.* She looked up. The grate over the top of the oubliette was a fair way above her. But if Jax had been in here, it would likely have brushed the top of her head, leaving her no room to move, as she wouldn't have been able to raise her arms, due to the physical constraints of the narrow sleeping chamber. Belinda turned in a circle. If she held her breath, she could even shimmy her arms up past her torso and lift them over her head.

She did so, and her fingertips brushed the grate. It began to open, sensing the bracelet, and she snatched her fingers back. *That's what you need to do,* she told herself. *Wait until the bracelet flashes red. At the last moment, reach your arms up, and use the bracelet to open the grate. As soon as the bracelet powers down for the night, run for it.*

No sooner had she thought the words, than her bracelet gave a quick vibration and began to glow red.

Chapter Nine

The lift groaned all the way to the upper decks. Clearly, it had fallen into disrepair after the barracks had been cleared out. Jax and the Doctor stood in silence, their hands clenched on the rails in a death-grip. Eventually, the lift ground to a halt, shuddering and wheezing like the last breaths of a dying man. The doors opened with a shrill grinding noise, and they found themselves at the bottom of a spiral staircase, just as Jax had said. It was rusted red, with steps missing, and ascended so high that they couldn't see the top of it.

'Wait,' Jax said. 'There's something you need to understand, before we go up there.'

The Doctor nodded. 'What is it, Jax?'

'It's about Vanessa. You know she was – *is* – my best friend.' A small smile crept across her face. Despite her muscular frame and towering height, she radiated a childlike joy at the mention of Vanessa. 'I remember the day she first told me about her "crime". It was six months into the cruise, and the first time I'd laughed since we set off. Vanessa was born to a family who ran a small space station in an asteroid belt. Her family had lived there for generations. There was a whole community of them on board, loads of families, all thriving in their own way. Then, one day, a mining company moved into the area, and started mining the asteroids for gas and precious metals. They were destroying the ecosystem of the belt – sending debris hurtling around the station at unsafe speeds. At one point, a piece of rock hit the station. The family that lived there . . . they died.' Jax swallowed, tears glimmering in her eyes. 'Vanessa launched her family's rickety old ship into the path of the next mining mission, and wouldn't move it. They tried to go round her, and she would zip in front to block their path. But obviously their tech was better, more advanced. They found a way round the stubborn girl in an ancient spaceship. But she didn't stop there. In the dead of night, she docked her ship to theirs and snuck on board. She found out they were occupying the asteroid belt illegally, and leaked the information to news sites. The company sued her family, and got her thrown in prison.' Jax shook her head, smiling in awe. 'That's the kind of person she is. And this was her punishment.'

The Doctor nodded slowly. 'Is that what you wanted to tell me?'

Jax shook her head. 'No. I just wanted you to understand.' Her fingers reached up towards her neck, worrying at the skin there. 'When I saw Martin, it all became so clear to me. Marilyn has taken enough – she has ruined enough lives, stolen enough futures.' She took a deep breath. 'So, I swore to myself that if I didn't find Vanessa alive, I would burn this entire cruise to the ground.'

Belinda ran for her life.

She had reached up as soon as the bracelet began to glow red, using the last of its life to slide open the grate above her head. Bracing her feet against the sides and pushing up, she scaled the walls in a crab-like stance. Her legs had burned with the effort, sweat breaking out over her forehead, until she had finally managed to hook her elbows over the top and haul herself out of the tiny chamber, inch by torturous inch.

She had stood there, waiting for someone to spot her, and taze her with an electric wire, but the bunkers had been deathly quiet. As soon as her bracelet had given one last buzz and gone dark – all trackers off, all reports to the central computer ceased – she had set off. Part of her felt guilty for leaving the other prisoners behind. But her best chance of helping them was to find the Doctor.

Her feet thudded against the ground as she ran through the corridors. She just needed to find the lift. *There*, they had come down that corridor, she recognised the sign.

A whirring noise echoed off the tall ceiling. *A mannequin, somewhere nearby.* She couldn't risk the lift, she realised – it was the main entry and exit point used by the sadistically creepy Marilyn-bots. Thinking quickly, and determined not to be slowed down, she took a turn at random. There had to be stairs. She didn't care if she was walking for seven days and nights just to get out of here – she would do it.

The air started to grow colder as she ran. Water dripped from the ceiling, landing in puddles that shone with the strange silver light that beamed in through the circular windows dotted high up, near the ceiling. When she came across a window at her head height, she half-expected to look out and see schools of silver fish flitting past, or sharks cutting through the water like dark grey knives.

The sight that greeted her was the opposite of that. An endless expanse of black – pure black, like a wash of fathomless shadow. Lights speckled the vastness like diamonds, colourful nebulae billowing throughout them like bolts of translucent silk thrown across the darkness. Her breath misted the glass, catching in her throat as emotion overwhelmed her. She felt so lost and alone.

Her fingers reached up to touch the glass. Was it possible she was looking at Earth right now? She had heard once that the distances between celestial bodies were so far that light took centuries to travel from one end of the galaxy to the other. Was it possible that one of these pinpricks of light was Earth? Was she looking at 2025 right now? Would she ever get back there? She sighed, dropping her hand. They'd got so close, so many times. But they'd also come so close to death. She remembered the bodies they'd seen on the diamond planet ... the pitched battle on Stenlar ... the casualties of the war on Missbelindachandra One ...

She stepped away from the window and faced the darkness. The only way to get home was to keep going.

There was no way to measure time passing. She began to keep track of her elevation, thinking that the more flights of stairs she climbed, the closer she would get to the main decks. It had taken a while to find a flight of stairs. For a few tense hours she had thought she would walk right down to the hull of the ship, and freeze to death. But, just as the cold was becoming unbearable, she had seen a rickety staircase. Slowly but surely, she'd grown warmer, and she thought it was a good sign when she saw the same white mushrooms she'd glimpsed on her way down to the bunkers. *Perhaps they only grow on certain levels – the ones at the right temperature. Which must mean I'm close to being back on the floor where the Doctor left me.*

She got off the staircase, venturing down one of the corridors. The mushrooms were thick along the sides of the corridors, and she had to step carefully to avoid them. To her dismay, they only became more and more common, until she was jumping from one bare patch of flooring to the next. She leapt again, and her foot slipped in a slimy puddle, crushing some of the mushroom.

A glowing plume of bright red smoke billowed upward. Yelping, she stepped backward, her foot landing in another patch of mushrooms. An even bigger plume erupted behind her, catching the bottom of her jacket. A crackling, popping noise followed, and the smell of cloth burning. Her jacket! She pulled it off, only to see the hem of it was black and charred as if it had been caught in a fire.

Horrified, she peered closer at the hazy smoke floating through the air. *Spores. Not smoke,* she realised. Each spore was tiny, and glowed red and orange as a flame. Nature's universal sign for *danger.*

Come back, Stenlar mushies, all is forgiven, thought Belinda.

Carefully, she draped her jacket over her shoulders, using it to cover her mouth and nose, in case she breathed in any spores. The soft tissue of her lungs did not need to be exposed to that. She'd learned many things on the A&E ward, but treating internal bleeding caused by burning alien fungus was not one of them.

Chapter Ten

Jax's words of vengeance rang in the Doctor's ears as they ascended the spiral staircase. She walked determinedly in front of him, while he lingered behind, mind going a million miles a minute as he tried to figure out how to fix things here. Jax had said that if she could not find Vanessa alive, she'd destroy everything. Clearly he wasn't about to let that happen. *Just find the central computer,* he thought, *use it to shut Belinda's bracelet down along with everything else.* All the prisoners would be freed. Perhaps they could even reach some kind of agreement with Marilyn. Right to clemency, better conditions, a paid salary . . .

The memory of the electric wires whipping out of the mannequin's torso flashed through his mind. Marilyn didn't seem like a woman open to compromise. Subtly, he pulled out the sonic and scanned their surroundings. The higher up they'd gone, the fewer holograms they'd encountered. That was a good thing. He buzzed the sonic again, re-triangulating their position to Belinda's and that of the central computer. The central computer was close by, and getting closer as they neared the upper decks.

To his dismay, however, he saw that Belinda had moved – covering an enormous distance since he had last checked. A few hours ago, she'd been so close by, still stranded in the middle levels of the ship. Now she was far below, about as deep as a person could get before the temperature got too cold. He watched the coordinates change again. She was on the move, at least, and gaining higher ground. *Hold on, Belinda,* he thought. *Just hold on.*

'Doctor!' Jax called. 'The door! It's here. Quickly, help me open it.'

The Doctor ran up the last few steps, rounding the final spiral. Jax was standing on the landing, her shoulder up against a door so thick it almost looked like they were inside a bank's vault.

'I think it's locked,' Jax said.

The Doctor made a show of stretching his arms. 'You'll want to stand back, babes.' He pointed the sonic at the door. The lock jumped, sizzling with a few errant sparks, before falling open with a satisfying *clank*. Jax wasted no time in grabbing the handle and pulling with all her might. The Doctor was right behind her, hauling at the door.

'Martin said the old crew barracks were empty.' Jax was breathing heavily with exertion. She leaned on the door, and it swung open easily. 'They should be just through here . . .' She trailed off.

The Moon Cruise

The door had opened into darkness. The Doctor had been expecting to see a disused room, rows of bunkbeds, stripped of sheets and personal belongings. He'd expected dust, and an easy way through. He should have known better.

The crew barracks hadn't been abandoned, they'd been repurposed. Stretching out in front of them, standing in neat rows, were hundreds of Marilyn mannequins.

'Don't move,' the Doctor said, his voice barely audible. 'Stay exactly where you are.'

Jax obeyed. 'Look at the eyes,' she said. 'In a room that dark, we should be able to see the scanners in their eyes. But there aren't any lights.'

The Doctor had noticed that too. 'But are they sleeping, or turned off? We know there are people inside ... maybe they also need to rest?'

Jax set her shoulders. 'Only one way to find out.' Before the Doctor could stop her, she hefted the broom into both hands and began walking slowly through the crowd of sleeping mannequins.

The mushroom spores clouded the air like tiny embers, glowing red and orange in the dark. Tears streamed down Belinda's cheeks. None of the spores had touched her, but they seemed to fill the air with noxious, peppery fumes that made her eyes smart like someone was cutting onions. She coughed, picking up the pace. Something soft squished under her foot, and she jumped back as a plume of stinging spores whooshed up like sparks from a bonfire. One of them caught on her sleeve. The fabric crackled, an acrid curl of smoke winding upward. Pulling her other sleeve over her hand, she patted the spores out. Her jacket and jeans were protecting her for now, but the spores were dangerous. At least they provided light – if the spores disappeared, she didn't know how she would see. This part of the ship's tunnels was clearly disused to the point of abandonment, and none of the lights worked.

After a time, much to Belinda's relief, fewer and fewer spores clouded the air. But the mushrooms seemed to be getting bigger the further she went. These larger ones were more domed on top, with hexagonal patterns stretching across them. They didn't seem to emit spores. Instead, they gave off a faint white light. Some were covered in a shiny, black chitinous substance, that looked hard to the touch. She didn't risk touching any of them, and stepped lightly around each one that bulged into the path.

She trudged on, cursing the Earth for disappearing, for making her journey back to it the long way round.

It was a strange bitterness – she couldn't honestly say she regretted any of it. The memory of stepping out into 1952 was one she'd never forget. The warm breeze around her shoulders, the way her yellow dress caught the evening sun . . .

A scuttling noise drew her out of her reverie. She

peered into the darkness. There was nothing there. It was probably a drop of water. The scuttling noise started again. Belinda whirled round, half-expecting to see a hideous creature behind her, but the enormous corridor was empty. Her only companions were the big glowing domes that seemed to grow out of the walls. She turned back, and her elbow bumped against one of them. It was slimy! Big clumps of mucus wiped off on her sleeve, clear and gloopy. She groaned in disgust, shaking her arm, but the stuff wouldn't budge.

Something strange was happening to the mushroom where she had touched it. She peered closer. It was a strange mushroom. It didn't have a stem, or any gills she could see. In fact, from this close up, it didn't look much like a mushroom at all.

The mushroom shook itself. Then the milky top layer split in half, retracting into the wall around it. Beneath that layer, the mushroom was moving, swivelling around. At the very centre of it was a red circle, with a black circle inside that. It darted all around the corridor, until it landed on Belinda. The black circle narrowed, as though focusing on her.

Belinda's jaw dropped. She stared, open-mouthed, in horror as the realisation washed over her.

The mushroom wasn't a mushroom. It was an *eye*.

All around her, the eyes were opening, a chain reaction started by her careless mistake of touching the one nearest her. Eyelids retracting, blinking away the mucus that had protected the eyes. Belinda backed away from the eye closest to her.

She needed to run, needed to escape. But one question was blaring through her mind: what kind of alien creature did these eyes belong to?

She didn't have to wait long to find out. With a roar, the entire wall slithered away. Belinda was knocked off her feet. An enormous column of scales ran past her, so quickly her hair blew back from her face. Thousands of scurrying legs clicked against the walls and the ceiling, as the insect-like thing roared its disapproval into the darkness. The shape of it became clear to her as it reared up. An enormous centipede. Its eyes were milky red. *It's blind,* she realised. That's why none of them had seen her as she walked amongst them. *That's* how she was able to get so far into this infested corridor without being detected; it was only when she'd touched one of its closed eyes that the beast had awoken. It squealed again, stamping the ground with hundreds of claws, before running over the ceiling and coming back down to face Belinda. It was as big as three double-decker buses, its body thick and muscular. How did centipedes kill their prey? Would it wind round her and squeeze until she suffocated? Or was the saliva currently dripping out of its maw and collecting on the hundreds of wiry hairs that protruded from its face a deadly poison that would kill or maim upon contact? Its eyes spun madly.

Belinda backed away.

She was done for. There was no other way to see it. She was going to die, ground up into mincemeat inside the mouth of an alien beast, or squeezed to death by its hundred flailing arms. Her brain was racing, trying to think of anything she could use as a weapon. But there was nothing.

Unless I use the spores, she thought. *No! I can't escape this new danger by plunging back into the old one.* But there was no time to think. The centipede was slithering towards her slowly. She was no fainting damsel. She was Belinda Chandra, A&E nurse. She had done worse, seen worse... removed worse from people's nether regions. This centipede would not be her cause of death.

Then the creature lunged. Belinda screamed, then turned as fast as she could. Grabbing her shirt front, she tugged it over her mouth and ran for the spores. She could hear the centipede behind her, gaining fast, scuttling over the floor, running up the walls and across the ceiling. Her breath was ragged in her chest. She wasn't sure if she was going to make it.

Her foot sank into a patch of mushrooms. *Whoosh!* A plume of orange spores shot straight upwards. She dodged, stepping on another, and another, then another. The spores rocketed up like geysers, spraying the centipede with burning specks of grit. The centipede screamed, thrashing in place, before scuttling on, roaring in pain. Belinda did not stop. Every step, more spores burst out into the air. The corridor behind her was thick with the stuff, and her own eyes were brimming with tears. Soon, she'd breathe some of the spores in, or get some in her eyes, and she'd be screaming in agony just like the centipede.

Hot breath blasted the back of her neck. She could hear the clicking of the centipede's mandibles, moments away from grabbing her.

Belinda stamped down with all her might. Glowing orange particles slammed right into the centipede's open mouth. Belinda dived, rolling across the ground. She stood up, watching in horror as the centipede shook its enormous head, its jaw unhinging and letting forth a terrifying howl. It fell off the ceiling and onto its back, its long body squirming, its legs wriggling helplessly. Belinda didn't stay to watch. On the opposite side of the corridor was a rusted door. She must have missed it before in the darkness, but the spores were everywhere now, and the corridor was bright as day. Drawing her jacket around herself, she ran over to the door, grabbed the handle and pulled with all her might.

Chapter Eleven

Mannequins surrounded the Doctor and Jax. He watched as Jax padded forward on the balls of her feet, moving surprisingly lightly for someone so tall. Neither of them dared to breathe as they moved through the lines of killing machines. The mannequins looked almost serene in their mechanical imitation of sleep, but their eyes were wide open.

The Doctor scanned them constantly, ready to run at the smallest flicker of red. He hated the thought of what was inside them. He could still hear Martin's final gurgling words. *Help me.*

What would really help was if he could remember what had happened to the Moon Cruise in the end. But the memory evaded him – too many regenerations had passed. When he looked up, he realised they were nearly at the end of the room. Carefully, Jax pressed the door open, stepping into the corridor beyond. The Doctor followed, closing the door behind him, inch by inch, until it shut with a barely audible click.

Neither of them spoke until they were well clear of the door. The next obstacle: navigating the upper decks.

The upper decks were more extravagant than the Doctor could have imagined. Clearly, they were reserved for the high-paying customers who doled out extra cash to experience the best the Moon Cruise had to offer. They had their own shops, their own spas, their own ballrooms and exclusive restaurants. For the entirety of the cruise's projected seventy-year journey, these customers would never venture to the lower sections.

Jax and the Doctor emerged from the barracks into a long corridor. The wealth and luxury of the upper decks was immediately apparent. Thick, soft carpets spilled across the floor in the same rich colour as red wine. Broad doors of dark wood were set into the wall every ten paces, concealing cabins that were no doubt ten times as spacious and well-appointed as the regular rooms on the floors below. Everything was gilded, or marble, or velvet. Easy-going laughter echoed from behind the closed doors, and soft music filtered through invisible speakers, so that it sounded like a string quartet was playing softly on every corner. They must have come out into the more residential halls, on the edge of the ship, far away from the central entertainment and leisure hubs.

'We need to get to the escape pods,' Jax murmured. 'They're well hidden, and all the intel I've heard from prisoners who used to work up here says they're underneath the stage in an auditorium located inside a sort of leisure and entertainment hub that they call the Clubhouse.' She gestured to a sign that pointed down the hall; its faintly glowing letters read CLUBHOUSE.

'What about escape pods on the lower levels?' the Doctor asked. It had only just occurred to him – surely there would be more on the lower decks.

Jax's face turned grave. 'We thought of that years ago. Word got sent out through the whisper network, encouraging all the other prisoners to try and find out the escape protocols and routes. Eventually, we did. A few brave souls snuck away to go and check if the routes were safe. Only a few of them made it back to us.'

'And?'

'Every single one was fake. Every exit sign led to nowhere, every tunnel leading to a crisis assembly point was a hologram, or a dead end. And not a single escape pod was located on the middle and lower decks.'

Footsteps interrupted them. Someone approaching round the corner. They bent their heads close together as if talking. A man in an extravagant suit came into view, arm in arm with a woman in a dress made entirely of violet feathers.

'We need to hide. *Quick!*' the Doctor hissed. They both looked around wildly, but there was nowhere to hide. Unless . . .

The Doctor pointed the sonic at the room closest to him. The lock flashed green and buzzed open. Grabbing

Jax's arm, he hauled her through, closing the door gently. For a moment, both of them braced to hear the shrieks of the room's potential inhabitants. Thankfully, none came. The plush room was quiet, if a little messy – dinner plates had been left on the side table, towelling robes flung over a low sofa. They were incredibly lucky that no one had been in.

A few tense moments later, the couple's footsteps passed by the room. Jax sagged against the wall in relief, but the Doctor's mind was whirring.

'We can't keep breaking into rooms to take cover – sooner or later, there'll be someone in one of them, and then our cover will be blown.' He paused. 'You said the escape pods are located inside the Clubhouse, yeah? That means we'll have to walk among the stakeholders. There'll be nowhere to hide. But it just might get me close enough to the central computer to shut down the bracelet system and save Belinda.'

Jax shook her head. 'We don't stand a chance, especially with me dressed in this.'

The Doctor walked over to the closet and threw it open. An assortment of ridiculously expensive clothing hung from the rack – silks that rippled like water, bejewelled skirts and tailored suits – and jewellery was piled on the shelves. 'We can fix that.'

Moments later, they exited the room, emerging back into the corridor. Both of them had been transformed. Jax wore a shimmery silver dress – the only garment long enough to cover her work boots – as well as a silk scarf to cover her bright green hair. The Doctor wore a new fur coat, a velvet top hat and a pair of gold-rimmed glasses to obscure his face.

He offered Jax his arm. 'Let's do this.'

Grimly, she accepted.

They walked swiftly through the carpeted corridors, following the softly glowing signs that pointed towards the Clubhouse. They were nearly at the end of the corridor when Jax stopped dead. More footsteps. The Doctor tensed, bracing for danger.

They turned to face the window. 'Rest your head on my shoulder,' Jax whispered. The Doctor did so. The footsteps grew nearer. Three ladies, laughing and talking, totally absorbed in the conversation. They passed Jax and the Doctor without a second glance.

The Doctor blew out a sigh of relief. 'We should hurry up,' he murmured. But beside him, Jax was wide eyed, drinking in the view, danger all but forgotten. 'I haven't seen the sky since I left home,' she breathed.

The Doctor felt a pang of sadness for her. 'The stars *are* my home,' he said softly.

'Pretty big home,' said Jax. 'Spring-cleaning must be a bind.'

He grinned at her. 'And the trouble is, I'm so house-proud!'

'Well, you should be. It's so beautiful.' Jax sighed.

'There aren't any windows in the shop, and we sleep underground. So the first thing Vanessa and I said we would do when we had escaped would be to find a place where we could see the sky. Somewhere away from the city. And we'd just sit there, looking up at it together.'

'Let's go and find her, then.'

There was a curious lack of television screens on the upper decks. On the middle decks, they'd been inescapable, constantly blaring, selling you a product or an experience. But up here it was quieter. Instead of flashing neon lights advertising new deals to entice customers, dark doorways beckoned and warm light diffused softly from tasteful sconces. Rather than broad walkways designed to allow as many people to shop as possible, the corridors on the upper decks were normal sized, as though they were in a swanky hotel in an upscale neighbourhood. It was clear that a different clientele lived on these decks – unlike the consumers on the floor below, who Marilyn was slowly draining of money, these people were tastemakers: investors, stakeholders, the ultra-rich. The galaxy's elite.

A few more inhabitants of the upper decks passed them in the low-lit hallways, but no one raised the alarm. Either the disguises were working, or perhaps no one on this level had even heard of Jax and the Doctor's escape attempt or their clash with the mannequins. Possibly Marilyn didn't want to worry her richest clients with anything other than the perfect experience she had promised them. Besides, if she admitted a worker had escaped and was running for their life, that would raise some uncomfortable questions about what they'd broken free from in the first place...

Soon voices reached them – the low din of a large crowd. The corridor opened up onto a balcony. Beneath them was the Clubhouse. It was an entire floor contained inside a perfect glass dome, surrounded by a balcony on all sides. Within it, the Doctor could make out different sections: restaurants and swimming pools, as well as a large theatre, slowly filling with people.

'There it is,' Jax said. 'The auditorium. The tunnel is under the stage.'

On the balcony opposite them, a set of solid gold doors had caught the Doctor's eye. Above the doors, a number was counting up. With a soft *ding*, the doors opened, and several security guards in black tuxedos stepped out. Above the lift, a camera swivelled slowly, following the group's progress down the hall.

Beside him, Jax was staring wide-eyed. 'Did you see those security guards?' She grabbed the Doctor, pointing at the lift. 'That has to be Marilyn's private lift. The high-speed one that can get you anywhere on the ship – any floor! – in a matter of minutes. Apparently it moves so fast, you have to strap yourself in or you could break your neck. I'd heard about it, but I'd never seen it before now.

'Interesting.' The Doctor made a mental note of its location. 'That might have to be my getaway car. After we find Vanessa, I'll come back here. I could get to Belinda in seconds. But for now we need to get into that auditorium.'

They watched from above as a snaking queue began to form outside the auditorium's doors. 'It seems like we'll be crashing the evening's entertainment.'

They took a spiral staircase down into the dome. Jax pulled her silky scarf lower over her face, and the Doctor made sure to tilt the brim of his hat downward, avoiding eye contact. Before they knew it, they were surrounded by upper-deck passengers, walking amongst them, trying to fit in. The Doctor felt like he was dangling above piranha-infested waters once again, but their disguises must have been so gaudy that they blended in with the rest of the clientele, as no one batted an eyelid at their presence. They made sure to keep their faces turned away from any cameras, Jax drawing the scarf even further over her head.

They walked quickly past a casino, where raucous laughter bounced off the walls. Tables of games seemed to stretch on for ever, croupiers trying to charm the passengers of the upper deck into a million ways to lose money or, as they put it, to *Take a chance on winning big!* There were restaurants serving every type of cuisine imaginable, one of them proudly displaying the carcass of an enormous deep-sea creature, halfway between an eel and a whale, splayed out on a bed of ice, its eyes misty, its mouth open to show its long, razor-sharp teeth.

The Moon Cruise

They averted their eyes, dodging the focus of the cameras as they made a beeline for the auditorium. The Doctor thought he heard a faint whirring noise, like a mannequin advancing at speed, but when he turned round, he only saw a spinning wheel of fortune, doling out luxury prizes to happy passengers of the upper decks.

Before long, they were standing at the back of a short queue that led to the auditorium's doors.

A doorman dressed in a suit and hat, with a shiny Moon Cruise pin in his lapel, stood in front of the door, checking invitations. They watched as a couple presented a plush white envelope, which the doorman opened to reveal an origami version of the cruise, the names of the invited attendees written across the side of it. Jax stopped short. 'We don't have an invite,' she murmured.

The Doctor took her arm. 'No, we have something better.'

The doorman smiled at them as they approached. The Doctor held up his psychic paper, lowering his head so the brim of his hat plunged the top half of his face into shadow.

The man squinted at it. He looked back up at them, his eyes narrowing further. 'One moment, please.'

Jax's grip on the Doctor's arm tightened.

The doorman waved over a colleague. 'Please, show him your invitation.'

The man leaned forward, reading whatever had appeared on the psychic paper. Within seconds, his eyes widened in shock. He shot a venomous look at his colleague, before bowing low, averting his eyes from their faces as he waved them through. 'Your Highness. Please, accept our sincerest apologies.' He leaned in a little closer and whispered conspiratorially, 'There are two vagrants on the run. We cannot be too careful. Please, enjoy your evening with Marilyn . . .'

'What just happened?' Jax whispered as soon as they passed him.

The Doctor winked at her, tucking the paper back inside his coat.

'I wonder what he means? "Enjoy your evening with Marilyn"?' Jax's hand on his arm tightened into a fist. 'If I see her, I'll –'

'You'll do nothing,' the Doctor said, calm but stern. 'You'll get to the escape pods, find Vanessa and leave. You'll go and see the stars, just like you promised her you would, remember?'

Jax deflated. 'Yeah,' she said. 'Yeah, you're right.'

The sounds of a lively evening soirée reached their ears, as they emerged from behind a curtain into some kind of gala – jazz music, laughter, the twinkling sound of glasses tapping together in toasts. A black and white chequered dance floor stretched out for many yards a glassy shining surface upon which couples danced to live music played by a ten-piece band. Everyone was dressed to the nines, ladies in gowns made of feathers and gold, fabric cinched and pulled, twisted and flared.

The men wore dinner suits, starched collars and coat tails, or long tunics that brushed the floor, so their slippers were visible. Diamonds and emeralds dripped from ears and throats, silver chains and gold bracelets adorned everyone from top to toe. The hairstyles were equally luxurious, with gemstones woven into braids, and tiaras made of gleaming metal. Even the band looked immaculate, their instruments shining in the low light.

'Music,' Jax breathed. 'Real music.' She was staring around in awe.

It occurred to the Doctor that all she had heard for the last six years were Marilyn's asinine infomercial jingles. 'Don't get distracted. We need to find a way to get underneath the stage.'

Before they could take another step into the room, a man walked across the stage, his shiny dress shoes tapping loudly over the hubbub of voices. His white-blond hair had been sculpted into a perfect set of old Hollywood-style waves, and his moustache was neatly clipped. The piercing eyes that stared out over his dazzling smile were a stunning shade of molten gold – contact lenses, perhaps. Above his head, a microphone descended from the ceiling. He grabbed it and tapped it three times. 'Is this thing on?' he joked, as his voice boomed throughout the hall. 'Thank you so much for joining us on this historic day. As many of you are aware, we have a visitor. This person is the one we have to thank for being able to host a soirée on a world-class cruise ship, and enjoy an experience afforded to less than 0.01 per cent of people in the galaxy – how exciting is that! I hope you've all enjoyed the drinks, and everyone better have tried the cod liver canapés.'

Jax made a gagging face.

'They're not bad,' the Doctor said, dabbing at his lips.

'But enough chatter,' the man went on. 'Everyone, please welcome to the stage a relentless innovator, a force of nature and, most importantly, the reason we are all here today, getting richer and richer without having to lift a finger! Everybody put your hands together for our truly inspirational leader, Marilyn Moon!'

Chapter Twelve

Rapturous applause echoed throughout the cavernous ballroom as Marilyn Moon made her big entrance.

She walked onto the stage like she had been born in high heels and a pinstriped suit, ready to exploit her fellow living creatures for profit. She smiled as though she could already imagine how much fun it would be to squeeze every single drop of money out of the audience in front of her, so that it could go straight into her own pockets.

Jax and the Doctor froze. All hope of getting underneath the stage to access the tunnel disappeared.

'Welcome to my cruise!' Marilyn threw out her arms. 'Aren't you glad you stopped by?'

'I LOVE YOU, MARILYN!' someone shouted from the audience.

She laughed indulgently. 'Of course you do.'

Everyone laughed. Jax scowled in disgust.

'Thank you for being here this evening. I have a few very exciting announcements.' Behind Marilyn, an enormous screen flickered to life. It was blank, until numbers appeared, flickering past, counting *up*.

The Doctor narrowed his eyes. The number was enormous, in the millions of billions, and it was growing every second.

'If that number means what I think it means ...' he said under his breath, but Marilyn had started up again.

'The number you see behind me, growing larger all the time?' She laughed. 'It's so enormous you can barely envision its magnitude.' Murmurs of agreement broke out. It *was* a nonsensical figure. Marilyn smiled, her mouth curved and sharp as a blade. 'This number represents the total profits that the Moon Cruise has taken since we set off on our voyage. This is not only generated by consumer spending but by advertising revenue and some very strategic product placement. Many of you will know that my company owns every single thing on board this ship. The movies the passengers watch are Moon Cruise productions; the screens they watch them on are made in my factories. All of which generates more money, which *all* flows back to you, my stakeholders, who receive a percentage of these profits!'

More deafening applause. Next to the Doctor, Jax was still, her eyes taking in that number.

'Does anyone have any questions? We welcome curiosity here at Moon Cruise Incorporated.' Marilyn's falsely bright tone suggested that the opposite was in fact true.

For a moment, it looked like she would get her way. But then a serious-looking man in a dark suit raised his hand. 'What about the rumours of bad treatment? I've heard that the Moon Cruise is being investigated by a humanitarian group. People who have worked here are coming forward and giving their stories. I've heard tales of overworking, punishment by electrocution and illegal contracts that never expire. Is there any truth to these rumours? And what are you doing to make sure Moon Cruise doesn't lose its shining reputation?'

Marilyn scowled. 'What a brilliant question.'

Jax's hand had flown to her mouth. Her eyes were shining with tears. 'They know,' the Doctor heard her whisper, more to herself than to him. He was taken aback by the sheer emotion and shock in her voice. 'Someone out there knows about us. Someone cares.'

In response to the stakeholder's question, Marilyn waved her hand. The screen changed to a picture of three prisoners in jumpsuits, silver bracelets on their wrists, smiling for the camera. 'You must be talking about the awful lies being spread about our rehabilitation programme. A programme that is the uncontested, most treasured *jewel* in the crown of the Moon Cruise enterprise. We are, first and foremost, a charitable organisation, and philanthropy is dear to my heart. Which is why I am so thrilled to be announcing a new project!' The screen flickered again. Behind her, a rotating model of a new piece of technology floated on screen. It looked like a highly sinister barcode scanner, with a grippable handle and a glass-fronted scanning mechanism.

'These rumours have been started against me by a vicious organisation calling themselves the Moon Cruise Investigation. The organisation is formed by ... ex-beneficiaries of the charity, who hold an inexplicable grudge against me, and are spreading lies about their supposed ill-treatment at my hands.'

'Escaped prisoners,' the Doctor surmised.

Jax nodded. 'Every year, a few brave prisoners make it out of the cruise,' she whispered. 'Most of them stow away on the supply ships that dock once every few months. I had *no idea* they were testifying against Marilyn to the Moon Cruise Investigation.'

Marilyn cleared her throat. The hubbub that had broken out at her mention of the Moon Cruise Investigation swiftly died. 'To protect the integrity of my brand, I have a new plan.' Her smile faded, her tone becoming more businesslike.

It was terrifying how quickly she switched between moods – playing the innocent ingénue, before revealing the razor-sharp intelligence beneath. That was a power that could have been used for good. *Why did she choose this?* the Doctor wondered. But he knew why. *Greed. Nothing is ever enough.*

'The Moon Cruise Investigation is an organisation that claims credibility through "first-hand accounts" and "eyewitness statements". We have reason to believe that this is a plot formed against us by our competitors.' A gasp rippled through the room. Marilyn nodded gravely. 'Indeed, we believe that our competitors are paying off ex-employees, bribing them to testify against us. They are using dangerous, illegal technologies to implant false memories in their minds, so that they hold up in questioning. It's barbaric, *reprehensible!*'

'Of *course* that's what it is,' Jax muttered.

'They seek to tear down everything we have built here! Everything that you, my dear stakeholders, treasured investors and precious passengers, have contributed to. Everything you enjoy, they want obliterated. But we won't stand for it!' Marilyn dabbed her eyes with a tissue – apparently overcome with emotion. 'Our plan is to stop the supply of their precious evidence. *How, Marilyn?* I hear you ask. It's simple. If there's no one who can testify to their experiences … the Moon Cruise Investigation will crumble. Every good investigator knows you need proof. We're going to eliminate their proof.' She gestured at the 3D model of the scanner on the enormous screen behind her.

Are my eyes playing tricks on me, or does it also look a bit like a gun? the Doctor thought. Unease spread through him as he leaned forward, trying to get an unobstructed look at the diagram through the crowd.

'This is a brand-new technology,' Marilyn explained. 'Created in my own personal laboratory over a period of several painstaking months, it uses wave therapy to directly stimulate the hippocampus, the part of the brain where memories are stored. In this way, memories can be targeted and removed with the simple press of a button.'

There was silence in the ballroom. Next to the Doctor, Jax was trembling with rage. He put a hand on her arm, whispering as quietly as possible, 'We need to bide our time and be careful. Things just got a lot more dangerous.'

'We've been trialling the technology, with great success, and I am pleased to announce that the first prototypes have officially been created.' From a drawer in the lectern, Marilyn drew out the real-world end product of the diagram above her on the screen. It was matte black, with the Moon Cruise Incorporated logo stamped on the side.

'Behold the means of these poor victims' deliverance,' she said.

Prickles ran down the Doctor's neck. He had no doubt the device had been made for crude efficiency – it would blast memories away without discernment, leaving a gaping psychic wound. The prisoners would always feel the lack of their past, the gap where memories should have been.

'Moreover, these devices have another use, just as kind and still more constructive.' The cameras flashed as Marilyn smiled even wider. 'We can remove all memories of past wrongdoings from the minds of our repurposed convicts. A fresh start with a cleaned-up mind. And I am ecstatic to announce that as of two weeks ago, construction has been completed on a brand-new cruise liner!'

Applause erupted, ecstatic smiles breaking out over the faces of the crowd.

'Since my mannequins are proving so popular and helpful on deck here, we have a surplus of staff. Therefore, the senior staff for the new cruise liner will be recruited from this very ship!' She waved her hands, and the screen changed. Suddenly hundreds of faces were flickering past, all of them in blue jumpsuits. 'We are transferring them for a deluxe memory cleanse as we speak. Soon, none of these convicts will remember the last seven years. They'll think they *just* boarded, excited and ready to start their new careers. A life of possibilities without end.' She winked. 'Quite literally, without end.'

There was a moment of quiet. The Doctor waited, bracing for objections, for someone to see through her soft-sell of her brutal programme, to recognise it for what it was and start shouting in outrage. *This isn't a fresh start, it's an extended sentence.* But they never did. Instead, rapturous applause broke out, deafening in intensity, until the very floor seemed to shake. A camera had picked up Marilyn's jubilant expression and projected it onto the big screen. She looked out at the audience, eyes roving from person to person, pure happiness radiating from her. Next to the Doctor, Jax had turned away from the stage in shock.

But the horrors weren't over yet.

Marilyn raised a hand, immediately silencing the

crowd. They leaned forward, not wanting to miss a word. 'I understand there may be sceptics among you. So allow me to demonstrate the capabilities of my new device. This morning, we captured an operative of the Moon Cruise Investigation – the puppet organisation created by our competitors to discredit us. She was skulking about by the escape pods, trying to gather intel on the cruise that she could twist and use to destroy our reputation.' A gasp rippled through the crowd. 'What you are about to see may shock you. They have convinced her that she was an exploited worker, trapped here and forced to work against her will for several years. Of course, that is nothing but a false memory implanted in her brain by the Investigation. A memory we will now cleanse her of, in front of all of you.' Marilyn looked sombre. 'Bring her to the stage.'

The centipede's dying screams faded to nothing as Belinda closed the door behind her. A single burning spore crept under the door, so she took off her jacket and wedged it in the gap.

What on earth was a giant centipede doing in the bowels of the ship? It had seemed right at home among the mushrooms and mould ... perhaps it was like an interstellar parasite, the kind of thing that started small and grew to an infestation if left unchecked. It happened in the hospital every few years – rats in the bins, biting mites in the waiting room carpets. Where there were large groups of people, creepy-crawlies soon followed. And in the dark, disused depths of a cruise across the galaxy, the creepy-crawlies were left to grow to epic proportions. She shivered, cold without her jacket. Wrapping her arms around herself, she took a look at her surroundings.

She seemed to be in some kind of workshop. Enormous machines were crammed into every corner. A half-fixed motherboard sat on one side of an old projector on a trolley. A dusty rack of cracked test tubes leaked purple fluid onto a table. A stack of cracked touchscreen tablets teetered on top of a workbench with an open toolbox underneath it. Luckily, the whole place looked totally abandoned. Pieces of old machines scattered the floor like so many rusted hunks of metal. Water dripped steadily from the ceiling, splashing onto old fast-food wrappers that Belinda recognised from the main concourse of the cruise.

Her foot nudged something, and it scraped across the floor. She looked down, and nearly screamed. A mannequin's dismembered head was staring up at her. It was half painted – only one ghoulish eye was blue, only half the mouth was red. The other half was totally blank. As though looking through new eyes, she cast another glance around the workshop. The mannequins were everywhere. Bits and pieces of them – unpainted faces and hands littered the floor. She even saw long spools of the deadly wire stacked up on top of each other. Maybe it was an old mannequin manufacturing workshop.

She walked further in, careful not to disturb anything. Other small details leapt out at her. A wrench left haphazardly next to a glass-screened tablet that turned on when Belinda tapped it, but only to a blank screen. She felt like the last person on Earth, walking among the ruins of its final civilisation. But it wasn't until she reached the centre of the workshop that she discovered an enormous map spread over the floor. She tilted her head, eyes widening when she realised it was a map of the ship, done in cross section, including floor plans of some of the levels. Her own location was circled in a messy red pen – labelled with the words, *I am here. I am always here.* It must have been left by the last inhabitant of the workshop.

With a shout of happiness, Belinda dropped to her knees and traced the path she had taken with her fingers. All the way from the service corridor where the TARDIS had landed to the sunglasses shop, and then down into the depths of the barracks. She had taken a left, away from the lift . . . Her finger dragged across the soft paper, her eyes widening as she saw how deep into the ship she had gone – how many flights down she had descended. For the first time, she allowed herself to acknowledge the aches and pains of her own exhausted body. Her throat felt like sandpaper, her knees were stiff. She lowered herself to the ground fully, sitting against an old chair. The map was a comfort. She cast another eye over it, trying to determine the best route back to the sunglasses shop.

She was certain that's where the Doctor and she would reunite.

Stay here was what he'd said. *Almost managed it*, she thought wryly.

Belinda shifted, trying to ease the pain in her back from climbing the stairs. Her elbow bumped something that made a sloshing noise. She turned, anticipating a spill. She caught the cup just in time. It was one of the huge containers for soft drinks; the passengers carried them everywhere. And this one was still cold! Her fingers wrapped around it; the cool condensation felt like heaven. She opened the lid, and saw glorious cubes of ice, and a pink drink that smelled like cinnamon bubblegum. Without a second thought, she began to drink it. The liquid was fizzy, the bubbles going straight to her head, the sugar deliciously sweet. She drained the whole cup and sat back, her eyes closed. This exhaustion was worse than the most brutal shift in A&E, and that was saying something. At least, back on Earth in 2025, she'd had her own room, a door between her and the rest of the world, a soft bed to lay her head down upon . . .

Belinda jolted awake. The cup had spilled ice across the floor. It was a melted puddle now, warm to the touch. What had woken her? The cup had spilled hours ago, from the looks of it. Stiff with sleep, she got to her feet.

Then it dawned on her. She had thought this place was abandoned, but the drink she had found . . . there had been ice in it. Which meant someone had left it there within the last hour or so, else it would have been melted when she first found it. Her heart squeezed with fear.

And the circle on the map, the words scrawled in red ink by a frantic hand.

I am here. I am always here.

She heard a door opening.

'Hello!' called a singsong voice. 'I'm home! Did you miss me?'

Chapter Thirteen

The door slammed shut. Belinda's heart jumped into her mouth.

'I said I'm ho-ome!' the singsong voice called out. It sounded almost childish, but it was too husky to be a child's voice. Belinda started edging backwards, then ducked behind a machine as she heard footsteps approaching. She had been through so much in the last twenty-four hours, she couldn't help but feel a tentative hope at the sound of another person's voice. Maybe the occupier of this workshop was another escaped prisoner, who hid here, away from the mannequins and the oubliettes, because it was the only place that was safe on the whole ship.

The footsteps rounded the corner. The person was humming, a lively, but lilting tune, one Belinda had never heard before.

'Did you miss me, my machines?' the person hummed. It sounded like a woman. 'Because I missed you – awfully! Terribly! I thought I might perish before I could hold you again!' The sound of long nails tapping against metal followed. 'I was out, sourcing parts. I have to scavenge them, but you know that. You're all in need of updates, and you won't fix yourself.' A more irritated note entered the woman's voice. 'Something big is happening today. I was supposed to receive three for transformations, but they've cancelled the order. I think *she* is scheming, planning something. But when is she not scheming?' Her voice became plaintive and sad. 'Perhaps if I'd noticed her scheming earlier, things might have been different.' There was a long silence. Then the woman gasped. Long nails squeaked against a drinks cup like nails along a blackboard.

'Who drank my lemonade?'

'Bring her to the stage!' Marilyn's voice rang out through the silent auditorium.

Two security guards appeared through a curtain at the back of the stage. Between them, a prisoner in a blue jumpsuit struggled feebly. A curtain of dark hair had escaped from her braid and hung over her face, obscuring it.

Next to the Doctor, Jax gave a strangled cry. '*Vanessa*. No!'

But her words were drowned out in the applause. The two security guards hauled Vanessa upright between them, before sitting her down on a chair. The cameras picked up her face, projecting it across the screens. Her eyes were rimmed red, but sleepy, as though she had been sedated. Her head lolled.

Jax turned to the Doctor. 'That's her. That's my Vanessa. Doctor, we have to do something.'

Marilyn picked up the memory-erasing device. 'I will now demonstrate the device's effects. With the click of a button, I can remove the false memories. This little spy won't remember a thing.'

'She's going to forget *everything*.' Jax was distraught. 'She's going to forget me.'

The Doctor was already pulling out the sonic. He turned to her. 'In a few moments, every single light in this auditorium is going to go out. The security guards will prioritise protecting Marilyn. You'll only have a few minutes to get onto that stage, get Vanessa and run.' He looked her in the eye. 'Get to the escape pods, and get out. Don't stop, don't look back. When you're safe, contact the Moon Cruise Investigation and help them spread the word of Marilyn's illegal activities.'

Jax was wide-eyed. 'What about you?'

Gently, the Doctor laid a hand on hers. 'Sometimes, our friends don't get to come with us on our next adventure. I'm going to stay here and save Belinda. But you have to leave while you can, Jax. Promise me you and Vanessa will try and get out?'

Tears welled in her eyes, but she nodded.

On stage, the security guards were strapping Vanessa

into the chair. Marilyn was walking toward her, a wicked glint in her eyes.

The Doctor gritted his teeth. 'Belinda's life and memories are at stake. I'm going to find her. I have to find her.'

'The lift!' Jax exclaimed. 'Marilyn's personal high-speed lift. It can go almost anywhere on the ship. Maybe you can use that to help you get closer to Belinda.'

'Jax, don't worry about me. Just get ready to run. You and Vanessa are about to see the stars again.'

On stage, Marilyn was raising the memory-erasing device. A cruel smile twisted across her face.

The Doctor did not give her time to pull the trigger. Silently, he lifted the sonic into the air. It buzzed, setting off a shower of sparks, as a concentrated electro-magnetic pulse short-circuited every single light in the auditorium.

The room plunged into darkness.

Chaos was immediate. On stage, Marilyn screamed. The Doctor felt Jax push past, weaving through the crowd to get to the stage.

'Help!' someone screamed. 'Help, I can't see!'

The Doctor didn't stick around to watch the carnage unfold. Already, people were pushing and shoving against one another, yelling in panic as the crowd crushed toward the exit. He was almost through the doors when the lights flickered back on. He stopped briefly in the doorway, casting one last glance back at the stage.

Marilyn cowered in a corner, surrounded by security

guards. She still held the unused memory-erasing gun in one hand, but the chair in the middle of the stage was empty, the straps undone. Vanessa and Jax were nowhere to be seen. For a brief moment, he thought he saw a low door underneath the stage close gently. *The tunnel to the escape pods.* Triumph swelled in his chest. *Safe travels, Jax*, he thought.

Marilyn's voice shrieked over the jostling of the terrified crowd. 'Where did she go? Find her! *Find her.*'

Turning round, the Doctor slipped through the doors, hat low over his eyes.

Belinda peeked out from behind the machines. A woman in a dark, tattered cloak was shuffling around the workshop. The hood was so low, she couldn't see her face. The woman hummed as she went around, cooing to the hulking, greasy machines as if they were the cutest puppies she'd ever seen.

'Did you miss me?' she tickled one on its robotic arm, *booped* another on its nozzle. 'I missed you, but I brought treats!'

Belinda backed further away. Was it better to stay in here or face the centipedes and spores again? The memories of the giant monster's mouth opening in front of her made her wince. She'd stay here . . . for now. Besides, maybe there was method in the apparent madness. There was a blood pressure monitor at the hospital; Belinda always had to ask nicely before she wrapped it around patients' arms, as it had been known to squeeze *way* too hard. And the vending machine! One nurse had told her you had to say please when you put your coins in, or it would refuse to release your chocolate bars.

The woman kept muttering, at times talking loudly to the machines – enquiries about their health, and the problems that had been plaguing them – and at other times whispering in a rasping monologue that did not cease. She barely stopped to breathe, just nattered on. Occasionally she would sing – jingles from the TVs that had played constantly in the glasses shop (and everywhere else around the ship, Belinda guessed). A lot of them praised Marilyn Moon, the woman whose portrait Belinda had seen in the storeroom, the lady in the pinstriped suit who seemed to be responsible for all of this.

Something brushed her ankle. Stifling a gasp, she turned round swiftly, only to see a soft pile of blankets and a thin pallet on the floor. The blankets were folded neatly on top of the thin mattress, the corners turned down like they would be in a hotel. *Or a cruise,* Belinda thought. Next to the bed were a line of neatly organised trinkets, tiny bits and pieces of machinery that had been salvaged and polished to a shine. A tiny pile of cogs was, on closer inspection, the back of a watch-face, frozen in time – perhaps snatched off the ground and saved from being crushed by the never-ending parade of passengers. Next to it lay a sparkplug, fastened to a small piece of corrugated iron. Its two prongs stuck out towards the bed, and held loops of metal – were they washers? Tiny sparkling pieces of coloured glass had been welded onto the tops of them so they looked like rings. *Jewellery,* Belinda realised. Maybe this wasn't the den of a madwoman but of a desperate person hiding from certain doom, trying to salvage enough to get by. There was even a small collection of bracelets, just like the one Jax had put over Belinda's wrist. But they were lifeless, turned off, sawed away down the middle. *She knows how to get them off!*

Spurred on by pure hope, and more than a little desperation, Belinda stepped round the machine. 'Hello?' she called out.

The muttering and clanking paused. 'Did you hear that?' the woman asked her machines. 'Who said that? Which one of you said that?'

'It wasn't them . . .' Belinda walked closer to the doorway of the other room. 'It was me.'

Through the door, the woman stood, facing away from Belinda. A long mane of tangled blonde hair fell down her back. Her legs were thin with malnourishment, and her clothes hung off her. She had been tinkering with something, but at the sound of Belinda's footsteps behind her, she froze.

Belinda pitched her voice softly, as if talking to a scared child. The woman began to tremble. She reminded Belinda of the children who were terrified to get injections or have their blood drawn. 'I mean you no harm. I just need your help.' If she thought it would have helped, she would have got down on her knees and begged. She was desperate. 'Please. I'm not supposed to have this bracelet on. I was tricked. But I outsmarted the oubliette, and evaded the killer spores. I even got past the gigantic centipede. I mean, most of all, I'm just glad to have escaped those hideous mannequins—'

The woman turned round. Her face was very familiar. A puff of wavy blonde hair, skin smooth, and eyes very wide and blue as sapphires. She had a streak of dark engine grease on her chin, and another splash on her forehead. Belinda was certain they had never met, but she looked so familiar...

The woman raised an eyebrow. 'Hideous? You think the mannequins are hideous?'

Belinda could do nothing but stare, as she realised why the woman looked so recognisable.

'But they're a copy of *me*.'

Alone now, the Doctor ran back the way he and Jax had come. A strangely tense atmosphere permeated the upper decks. On their way in, total calm had suffused the space. Now, an atmosphere of barely suppressed fear set him on edge. His eyes darted around, observing everything. It didn't seem to be coming from the patrons themselves. They were kicking back, with drinks in hand, relaxing and laughing, playing pool, or making their way at a leisurely pace over to the cinema. A pair of stakeholders walked in front of the Doctor in nothing but their swimming costumes, hats and goggles, towels thrown over their shoulders – the picture of relaxation.

No, the sense of terror was coming from the crew members.

He passed a bar. In front of it, a young man in an usher's uniform was whispering to the two bartenders. 'She's going to erase our memories. I heard it, plain as day. She tried to sell it to the investors as some story about a competing firm. But none of it was true.'

The Doctor recognised him. He had been handing out canapés in the auditorium. He must have heard everything. There had been more crew members present in the auditorium – one to hand Marilyn her microphone, another to tick names off on the door . . .

As the Doctor watched, one of the bartenders picked up a walkie-talkie and began murmuring into it, no doubt trying to find out further information from the network of upper-deck workers.

The Doctor smiled to himself. It was like watching fire flickering in the kindling of a bonfire. Marilyn had treated them like less than nothing for so long that she had stopped being able to see them. In her eyes, they were powerless, and so they had become totally invisible to her. But her carelessness might have cost her everything.

On an instinct the Doctor pointed the sonic at the

walkie-talkie, opening the broadcast channel, so that anyone with a walkie-talkie would hear the young man's account of the events in the auditorium. If the flames of resistance were catching, he had just fanned them into what could become an inferno.

He hurried back through the casino, head low as he reached the staircase that would take him back up to the balcony. He was headed for Marilyn's private lift. It was likely that the lift ran on a specialised track, one that regular lifts could not use. If his suspicions were correct, and the sonic was up to the task, he could chart a new course using the pre-existing network of elevator shafts, and use it to get to Belinda. He checked the sonic. Her location was mystifying. She was deep in the lower decks, almost beneath them. He hated to think what had drawn her down there.

At the top of the staircase, the Doctor stopped dead. Two ushers were posted outside the golden doors. But instead of standing guard, they were huddled round a telephone that was attached to the wall. A crackly voice was coming out of it.

'. . . *erase our memories. I repeat, Marilyn is planning to erase our memories.*'

Before the Doctor could even approach the lift, the two workers bent their heads together, arguing. He paused behind a corner.

'If that's true, I'm not waiting for it to happen to me,' one of them said. 'You heard him, she's going to erase our memories, and send us to another ship. If she gets her way, we'll be here for ever.'

'But what if—'

'I'm tired of waiting for someone to come and save us. Maybe we need to save ourselves.'

The younger usher took off, walking swiftly down the corridor. After a moment's hesitation, the older one followed.

The Doctor darted out from behind the corner, pointing his sonic at the doors. They shuddered open with a creak and a groan. With another click of the sonic, the doors slid shut. Belinda was a very long way away but, according to Jax, this lift was incredibly fast – a fact corroborated by the row of four seats inside it, complete with seatbelts to secure the inhabitants against G-forces as the lift descended at an incredibly high velocity. The panel of buttons stretched across the entire wall. Every single deck was accessible. It was chilling, the Doctor thought, that Marilyn could be anywhere in the cruise in a matter of seconds. He had better hurry up. It wouldn't take long for her security to realise the lift had been hijacked.

According to the sonic, Belinda was somewhere between the twelfth and thirteenth floors. The upper decks were floors 209–215. He had a long way to go. Without hesitation, he jumped into one of the seats, strapped himself in and pressed button 12.

The lift gave an enormous shudder and plummeted downward.

The Doctor *whooped*, throwing his hands up like he was on the best roller-coaster ride at the best theme park in the universe. 'Now *that's* what I'm talking about!' The lift shot to the side, then went straight down, then launched itself sideways again before continuing its rapid descent. The numbers on the dial were falling fast.

He was around floor 87 when the speakers crackled to life.

'ATTENTION, CREW MEMBERS. THERE ARE HOSTILE INTRUDERS ON BOARD THE SHIP. MAKE EVERY EFFORT TO DETAIN THEM, AND YOU WILL BE REWARDED.'

The numbers fell faster as the lift descended. 53, 52, 51 ...

The lift slowed ... 13, 12 ... before coming to a smooth stop.

The doors dinged open and a cold blast of freezing air hit the Doctor in the face.

The corridor that stretched out in front of him couldn't have been more different to the middle and upper decks. Belinda had travelled well below decks. It was dank and cold down here, the ceilings dripping with water, the floor covered in murky sludge.

He felt another pang of guilt at the thought of Belinda stumbling through corridors like these, alone and scared. She had made the smart decision, though. There were no cameras or mannequins of any kind to be seen down here. The only enemy was the dark and the damp. And if he knew one thing about Belinda Chandra, she would have put up a good fight.

'Hold on, Belinda,' the Doctor whispered, as he set foot into the dark. His voice bounced off the walls, so that it sounded like a thousand ghosts repeating his words back to him. 'I'm going to find you.'

Chapter Fourteen

Belinda gaped. The woman before her was Marilyn Moon.

'Surprised to see me down here?' Marilyn smiled. It was the same smile Belinda had seen on the portrait – broad and warm but a little too tight. A smile that said, *Give me all your money, I'll keep it safe. Promise.*

Belinda didn't respond. Instead, she started backing away. Slowly.

Marilyn shook her head, a maniacal glint in her eye. She muttered something too low for Belinda to hear.

Belinda hesitated.

Something was off. Why would Marilyn be in this room? With its tiny, sad bed, and the nuts and bolts for jewellery? Why were her clothes in rags – where was the famous red and white pinstriped suit?

'Why *are* you down here?'

'How dare you question me like that!' Marilyn exclaimed. Belinda's heart dropped into her stomach. But then Marilyn – or whoever this woman was – collapsed into a fit of giggles. She laughed so hard, she bent double, slapping her knee with her hand.

'Are you all right?' Belinda asked.

But the woman only screeched another laugh, wiping tears from her eyes. 'At least, that's what I *imagine* Marilyn would say.' She shrugged. 'I wouldn't know, we haven't spoken in years.'

'But you look just like her!' Belinda couldn't stop the words from tumbling out. 'You're literally identical. Are you, like, twins?'

The woman had lost interest in Belinda now that she was no longer playing tricks on her, and was bustling around the machines, talking to them. 'Well, almost.' Marilyn's doppelgänger bent down to a small machine, cupping her hand over her mouth to whisper to it. 'Shall we tell her the story?' Another giggle. 'Shall we start with "Once upon a time"?'

'You don't have to explain. I was actually hoping you could tell me how you got all those bracelets off—'

'Oh, *fine*, we'll tell you.' Not-Marilyn flopped into a chair. 'My name is Monroe. It's Marilyn's joke – about a funny little film star from a very long time ago.'

'Yeah,' Belinda said faintly. 'I'm familiar.'

'I'm not her twin – I *am* her.' She waved a hand at the broken parts of the Marilyn mannequins that littered the floor. 'I was an early prototype. A solution to the problem of enforcing Marilyn's laws and guarding the prisoners – I mean, "crew members",' she added with a sarcastic grin. 'She wanted to make her presence felt everywhere. I remember, when she made me, she said, "I want to be *inescapable*."'

'When she made you?'

'Oh yes. She cooked me up in a lab. I was made from a single strand of her hair. A perfect clone. That's what she wanted. There was going to be one of me in every shop, as a manager. She was a genius. Why trust someone else to do it, when you could do it yourself? She wanted a thousand perfect servants, who could do her bidding faultlessly. Instead, she got me. Another Marilyn, just as ambitious, just as willing to do whatever it took to achieve my goals. Just as cutthroat. And I wasn't content serving her every whim.'

Belinda took another tiny step back. The centipede wasn't looking quite so bad now. 'But why are you down here? What happened?'

'She got insecure. Sad, really.' Monroe shook her head. 'Also, I tried to kill her. So she locked me down here, below decks, in the dark depths of her cruise ship, so far down that even the light doesn't reach.' She sighed and looked lovingly towards her machines. 'At least she gave me a purpose. For that at least, I have her to thank.'

Belinda took a second look at the machine that took up most of the centre of the room. She was staring at the back of it, she realised – the tangle of wires was wrapped around a central chamber, the front of which she could not see. 'You make the mannequins.'

Monroe grinned. 'I do. Would you like to take a look at my machine? You're about to become *very* familiar with it, after all.'

Warily, Belinda nodded. With slow steps, she walked over to the machine. Behind her, Monroe had started laughing uncontrollably, her thin frame wracked by a high-pitched fit of giggles she was attempting to smother with her hand.

On the side of the machine was a separate compartment. Inside was a Marilyn mannequin. Its wooden exterior was fresh and new. The paint on it still looked wet to the touch, as if it had only been finished a few hours ago and had been left to dry. It looked exactly like the one that had detained Belinda in the sunglasses shop, the same as the one that had electroshocked her and led her to the oubliette. The same as the hundreds of other mannequins that patrolled the cruise like security guards in a shopping mall. There was only one difference between this one and those.

The head had not yet been finished. The front half of it was missing. And in the space underneath, Belinda saw the secret of the mannequins.

A young man's face stared back at her, his skin grey and sallow, his eyes blinking slowly. A tangle of viscera was entwined around a column of wires – no doubt the conduits for his life force, being sapped away to create a creature halfway between a man and a mannequin. Belinda's hands shook as they came up to cover her mouth.

Beside the creature lay the wooden shell of the face that was yet to be attached. Its blue eyes stared at the ceiling, unseeing. The mouth, with its hinges that mimicked the look of speech, was open, as though the face had been frozen in a silent scream.

Belinda froze. There was not a single doubt in her mind that Monroe was going to try and turn her into a mannequin. Her voice was a terrified whisper as she turned around to face the clone. 'Please, just let me leave. I won't tell anyone what you're doing. Just let me out.'

Monroe giggled. 'Can't you see, it's far too late for that? I'm going to give you a makeover!'

'You're a *monster.*'

Monroe looked at Belinda, plaintive as a child. 'No, no. You don't understand. The mannequins are going to be our salvation. They're going to help me stop Marilyn.' Her eyes lit up. 'They're going to help me get revenge.'

Belinda stared. 'Revenge?' Her heart was pounding. 'How is turning innocent people into mannequins going to help you get revenge against Marilyn?'

'Oh, you'll never guess!' Monroe spun in a giddy circle. 'But since you asked . . .' She gestured to the pile of bracelets, then pointed to the buckets of paint – yellow for the hair, blue for the eyes, pale orange for the skin, and red for the suit – and the blocks of timber, ready to be inserted into the machine and carved up into mannequins. 'My dear sister Marilyn left me in charge of programming the mannequins. And what she doesn't know is that there is a protocol buried deep within their brains. One that I put there. And one day, when I have made enough mannequins to be certain of my victory, I will activate the protocol. The mannequins will become an army, believing Marilyn is the enemy that must be subdued. They will stop at nothing to achieve that goal. And anyone who gets in their way?' Monroe drew a line across her neck. 'Isn't that genius?'

'The cruise will become a warzone,' Belinda pointed out.

Monroe stiffened. 'Not if everyone agrees with me. Which I'm certain they will.'

'You don't *sound* certain.'

'Well . . . I . . .'

An idea flashed through Belinda's mind. *Keep her talking. Bide your time.* 'What if I could help?' She pointed to the machine. 'The prisoners. You need them on your side, trust me. If Marilyn can convince them to protect her, you'll never find her. How many mannequins have you made?'

'Hundreds!'

'It won't be enough. There are more prisoners than mannequins.'

'That's why I'm making more, starting with you.'

'No!' Belinda said too hastily. She paused, thinking on her feet. 'It would be a waste to turn me into a mannequin, because I am a valuable asset. *I can help you.* I know what their conditions are like, I understand their grievances and their way of life. I could bargain with them on your behalf. I could win them over to your side. It won't take much. They hate Marilyn already.'

Monroe looked thoughtful.

'But it won't work if I'm a cyborg mannequin,' Belinda insisted. 'They won't trust me.'

Monroe was shaking her head. 'It's not the right time. I have to strike while she least expects it, or she'll overwhelm me instantly.' She looked longingly at the machine. 'I'd rather keep on building my army. Starting with you.' She lunged forward, grabbing Belinda by the wrist.

'Get off me!' Belinda tried to yank her hand out of Monroe's grip, but the clone's hand was murderously tight. 'Let go!'

Monroe didn't seem to hear her. She started humming another jingle, viciously pulling Belinda over to the front of the machine, where a long, coffin-like chamber with a circular window on the front awaited her.

Belinda began to fight, yanking her arm away as hard as she could. Her shoulder socket burned in agony as she ground her feet in. Monroe's nails dug into her wrist as she hauled her forward.

'Get off me!'

Monroe reached over to a side table and grabbed hold of a drill. With a smile, she turned it on. The long, rusted drill bit began spinning, whirring menacingly. She pointed it at Belinda's head. 'Get in the chamber.'

Terrified, Belinda began walking towards the machine.

Was this how it all ended? Would she never get back home? Would she die here, transformed into a mannequin, brainwashed into becoming part of Monroe's cyborg army?

'You're going to be snug as a bug in a rug in there!' Monroe giggled, the drill in her hand whirring even faster. As Belinda got closer, she realised the rust on it was mixed with old, dried blood. 'Just step right in.'

In the distance, Belinda heard a very familiar noise. A whining buzz that triggered memories of a kind smile and clever eyes. Someone who never led her into danger on purpose, and who always made sure she got out alive.

The door to the workshop crashed inwards in a billow of dust. Paint buckets splattered, mannequins collapsed like dominoes and Monroe screamed as a figure stepped through the cloudy air.

Belinda felt relief flood through her. 'Doctor!'

Chapter Fifteen

'Belinda!' The Doctor rushed forward.

Monroe's grip only tightened as she pushed Belinda in between herself and the door, using her as a human shield. She revved the drill. 'Get back!'

The Doctor stopped short at the sight of Monroe and the drill. Despite being held hostage, Belinda could have cried with relief to see his face again. It was only now that he was back that she allowed herself to admit there had been multiple times when she truly wasn't sure if she was going to make it out of here alive.

'Who are you?' screeched Monroe.

The Doctor's eyes widened as he took in her face. *You. But . . . you're not you.*' He looked between Belinda and Monroe, clearly trying to understand how Marilyn Moon could be standing in front of him in this dank underground dungeon of a workshop.

'Evil clone,' Belinda explained succinctly. 'She turns prisoners into mannequins. Now she wants to raise a mannequin army against the real Marilyn – also evil.'

'Efficient,' the Doctor replied.

'Shut up!' Monroe yelled. 'I'm not evil. I'm the one who's been wronged, can't you see? I'm only trying to do what's best for everyone.'

The Doctor narrowed his eyes. 'Done nothing wrong? You've killed hundreds of people by turning them into mannequins.'

'They aren't dead, they're just . . . different.' Monroe's grip on Belinda's arm loosened as she tried to justify herself. 'I've never killed a soul.'

Keep talking, Doctor, Belinda thought. *She's easily distracted.*

The Doctor stepped in. 'You say you've never killed anyone, but what kind of a life do you leave for them? One with no memory of who they were? Just a face, detached from a real body, stuck inside a wooden cage like a sinister theme park character? A life where they have to work for ever for the very woman who sold them a dream in the first place?'

Monroe stepped back a little, cowering beneath his gaze, her hand almost releasing Belinda's arm.

'I travelled to the upper decks, you know,' the Doctor went on. 'We heard Marilyn speak. She told everyone about her plan for a new cruise, a way to "recycle" workers. She's created a memory-erasing gun that targets the brain and can induce selective amnesia. Make people forget who they are, so they can continue serving the cruise.' He feigned thought, tapping his chin. Belinda knew that look. He shrugged. 'Sounds like you two aren't as different as you thought.'

Monroe's face crumpled in shock. She let go of Belinda, stepping round her to advance upon the Doctor. 'We *are* different!' she insisted, brandishing the drill at him.

Belinda stood still, praying that Monroe would not notice she had let her go.

'Are you?' The Doctor peered at Monroe, unrelenting in his cross-examination. 'Or are you just mad and sad that you aren't the one with the power?'

Monroe opened her mouth to reply, but no words came out. She hugged herself around the middle and began rocking back and forth. 'I am here,' she whispered to herself. 'I am always here. I am here. I am always here.'

The words from the map. A madwoman's scrawl, Belinda had thought. But also, she realised, a way for Monroe to remind herself she existed. To comfort herself in the dark depths of the workshop Marilyn had confined her to.

Belinda stepped forward. Beneath her feet, an old piece of timber snapped.

Monroe spun round, a feral glint in her eye. 'Get in the machine!' She lurched towards Belinda, but the Doctor was faster.

'Get away from her!' he roared.

Monroe lunged again but, this time, Belinda was prepared. She held her hands out in front of her, shoving

Monroe away. Quick as lightning, the Doctor kicked a low box so that it slid across the floor, landing behind the clone.

Monroe's arms pinwheeled as her calf collided with the box, but it wasn't enough to stabilise her. With a scream, she fell backwards into the coffin-like chamber.

Its door closed with a hydraulic *hiss*, sealing automatically over her.

Monroe banged on the door, tiny fists raining down on the thick glass. Her eyes were wild, glazed over with panic and hatred. Her mouth made the shapes of sounds, but the glass was so thick, barely anything came out.

'Doctor . . .' Belinda let out a stuttering sigh of relief. Her knees felt weak. She could scarcely believe that the turmoil was over, that there was no immediate danger. The Doctor ran over to her, catching her as her legs buckled beneath her. She buried her face in his shoulder, trying to hold back tears of relief. 'I thought I'd never see you again.'

He grabbed her by the shoulders, allowing her to lean on him until she felt strong enough to stand on her own. 'Belinda, I would never stop until I found you. Do you understand?'

She nodded, smiling gratefully. 'Can we go home now?'

'We can try our best.' The Doctor grinned.

Monroe slammed her fists on the glass. 'Let me out!' Her voice was muffled.

'What should we do?' Belinda asked. 'It feels . . . bad

somehow to keep her in there. I know she did wrong, but...'

'She did more than wrong,' the Doctor said, his expression dark. 'She nearly killed you, like she's already killed hundreds, turning them into monstrous soldiers for her mannequin army. All to serve her personal vendetta. Revenge. Well, this is mine. We'll leave her in there until her sister arrives.'

Monroe thrashed harder. 'No! Anyone but her, anyone but her.'

The Doctor walked over to the window, ignoring her. 'The door can be released on a timer. We should set it now, and get out while we still can. I have a feeling the Moon Cruise is not going to be a tranquil oasis for much longer.'

'No!' she screamed. 'Don't leave me. *Please don't leave me alone with my sister!*' She slammed her fist repeatedly into the glass.

There was a sudden series of frenzied beeps. Text scrolled across the top of the machine:

PRISONER RESISTANCE DETECTED
EMERGENCY PROTOCOL ACTIVATED
TRANSFORMING SEQUENCE BEGINNING

Monroe hit the glass one last time. The text changed:

TRANSFORMATION INITIATED

A low vibration started, a barely audible hum that they felt more than heard. The enormous machine drawing power into itself. The glass frosted over.

The Doctor leapt into action, pressing buttons on the front of it, pulling levers, trying to stop the process from completing. But the vibration soon became a shuddering jolting, as the machine leapt into a higher gear. A sheet of metal descended over the chamber's window, and a sound like a meat grinder started, a relentless churning of gears, interspersed with wet popping sounds. The Doctor smacked the machine with his palm in frustration.

Belinda pulled him away. 'It's too late.'

They watched in shocked silence as Monroe became a victim of her own twisted experiments. Belinda closed her eyes. She couldn't watch. *I am here*, the mad clone had whispered to herself. *I am always here*. And now she always would be.

'Let's go,' the Doctor said, stepping away from the machine. 'I don't want to be here when she pops out of it as a mannequin.'

Without Monroe, the workshop had suddenly become darker and more sinister.

Belinda nodded. 'I'm more than ready to go home.' *Understatement of the century.* 'It feels like it's been *days* since I last slept—'

The door to the workshop burst open. The Doctor and Belinda jumped back as several mannequins whirred into the workshop, electric wires crackling, ready to launch.

Behind them strolled in the real Marilyn, her heels clicking on the ground.

Seeing her in the flesh was surreal – Belinda felt like a fool for ever mistaking Monroe for the woman she had been cloned from. Marilyn was perfect. Her hair and skin shone with good health, her nails were flawlessly manicured, her heels the ideal height. Even her red and white pinstriped skirt suit, which should have been hideous, fitted her like a second skin, lending her an aura of power that had Belinda shrinking back against the wall.

The machine kept grinding and popping, turning Monroe into a mannequin. Marilyn spared it no more than a glance. 'What a shame,' she murmured. She picked an invisible piece of lint off her skirt's hem. 'She did have her uses.' Levelling Belinda and the Doctor with a gaze that could have melted through iron, she purred, 'Not sure if I could say the same about you.' Belinda noticed she was wearing a red leather holster on one hip. Was she armed?

'So,' Marilyn said, folding her arms over one another. 'Be honest, did you really think I would let you get away with this?' She undid the holster at her waist, her long fingers deftly unbuckling it and withdrawing a strange object that looked almost like a gun, if not for the slim glass panel on the front of it. She held it casually in one hand, as if it were a wine glass, or a bouquet of flowers.

Beside her, the Doctor went rigid. 'Belinda,' he warned, 'if that thing hits you, you'll lose all your memories.'

'Oh no,' Marilyn pouted. 'You ruined the surprise.' She shrugged. 'Ah well. It's not like you'll remember it anyway.'

She was so blasé. Horror gripped Belinda. *A memory-erasing gun?*

Marilyn kept talking, waving the gun around like it was nothing, and not the most terrifying weapon Belinda had ever seen. 'Now, I've been doing this job a long time,' the woman said. 'And during that time, I've learned a few things. It turns out rebellions are similar to weeds. It's not enough to cut them off above ground. You have to uproot them at the source.' She raised her voice towards the open doorway. 'Bring them in.'

A pair of security mannequins escorted two people into the workshop. The captives were bound and gagged, both of them terrified. Belinda's eyes widened. They were the two workers who had got her into this predicament in the first place. Jax and Vanessa.

'Jax, no,' the Doctor breathed. 'What happened?'

Marilyn threw back her head and laughed. 'What happened is that none of you are as clever as you think you are. You must think I'm stupid, that I wouldn't put two and two together. I figured out very quickly that you were all working together. And since you're all so close, I thought I'd at least give you each the privilege of watching your friends forget that you ever existed.' Marilyn turned the gun on the Doctor. 'You first.'

Belinda watched Marilyn pull the trigger. The cruel twist of her mouth, the casual press of her finger against the ray's strange handle. The barrel glowed with light before firing a single bright bolt. *It doesn't matter if I forget,* she thought. *This isn't my life.*

Belinda threw herself in front of the Doctor. Her arms came up on instinct to shield her face, her shoulders bunched up by her ears in fright. She heard screaming.

More than anything, she hoped she would wake back up in the TARDIS with no memory of anything that had happened. Maybe the amnesia would even last until she was home, and all she would remember were the robots in the hallway of the house-share, and then... nothing.

All gone like a bad dream.

Of course, it also meant she would lose all the good bits. The laughs she'd had with the Doctor, the first time she'd stepped out of the TARDIS into another time, wearing that incredible yellow dress. She'd forget the things she'd seen – planets and galaxies and asteroid belts; the perfect velvety darkness of space, stars splashed across it like a spill of diamonds. She'd forget all the victories, too. All the times she'd surprised herself, by being bold, or smart, piecing things together before the Doctor did. She wouldn't remember all the times she'd helped people, which was sad because she loved helping people more than anything, though she rarely admitted it.

All of it would be gone. The good and the bad. The devastating and the brilliant.

Belinda's hands shielded her face. Something hit

her wrist, boiling hot, like she had put her hands close to a flame.

She looked up through the cracks in her fingers, tried to recall the last few days. It was all there, she was sure of it; the bolt hadn't taken anything.

But if it hadn't hit her, who had it hit?

Marilyn lay in a heap on the floor. The gun had flown out of her hand, bouncing a few feet away. Her eyes were open, glowing with a strange white light. Belinda lowered her arms in shock.

'The bolt hit her,' the Doctor said in wonder. 'Your bracelet deflected the bolt, and it hit Marilyn instead.'

'Surrender now, or face the maximum sentencing.' The mannequins beside Marilyn were still active, electric wires unspooling from their hidden compartment.

Jax dived for the memory ray, grabbing it off the floor. She turned round, shooting it twice. Each bolt hit one of the mannequins. As soon as the ray made contact, the mannequins became disoriented, whirring about mindlessly, bumping into each other and crashing into walls. Jax dropped the gun, clearly in shock at her own actions. But she'd saved them. If she hadn't acted so quickly, the mannequins would have electrocuted them all.

The Doctor ran over to where Marilyn lay. He picked up the gun between thumb and forefinger like it was a dirty sock. 'I'll be having you,' he said, and tucked it away in an inside pocket. Then he touched Marilyn's shoulder. 'Can you hear me?'

'Urghh,' she groaned. The glow faded from her eyes. She sat up blearily, resting on her elbows. A lock of blonde hair fell across her face. 'Where am I?'

Before anyone could respond, Jax pointed at Belinda's bracelet. 'Belinda, look!'

The bracelet was vibrating, cycling through its different colours, blue, red, white, green. Then the screen went black. The number of years left on the sentence started scrolling down, from 78 to 65, to 41, and 30, to 20 . . . to zero. It gave one last vibration. Two words scrolled across the screen. SENTENCE COMPLETED. An invisible hinge opened, and the entire thing slid off Belinda's arm and clattered to the floor.

'What happened?' Belinda asked, mystified.

The Doctor grinned. 'The bracelet forgot its purpose. Or, in technological terms, everything was deleted. Total system reboot.' Seeing Belinda's expression, he elaborated. 'Brains are just incredibly complex computers – if the gun can alter or entirely remove the memories of a human being, why not the memories of a machine?'

Belinda rubbed her wrist, just grateful to be free of the bracelet. She turned back to Jax and Vanessa. Their expressions were sheepish. 'I'm glad you two found each other, I am. But did you have to drag me into this mess?'

They looked at the floor, ashamed. Jax was the first to speak. 'I'm so sorry, Belinda. What I did was wrong. But I did what I thought I had to do to escape. We've been trapped here for six years. We thought we'd spend our whole lives as prisoners of Marilyn Moon.'

'Who is Marilyn Moon?' came a confused voice. On the floor, the lady in question was struggling into a sitting position. Her hair was frazzled and her skirt suit was knocked askew. She looked very far from the polished, perfect billionaire cruise owner Belinda had first seen on television. 'And why on earth has she been holding people hostage?'

Chapter Sixteen

They all stared at Marilyn.

'Someone will be down here soon to come and find her,' Jax said uneasily. 'We should go.'

But the Doctor held up his hand. 'Wait, I have a better idea.' He walked over to the large wall of computer monitors. 'If we just ...' His hands flew over the keyboard, typing so fast Belinda couldn't make out a single word. He tapped a few more buttons and adjusted a webcam. The screens suddenly flickered to life, all filled with the Doctor's face.

'In a few seconds, this will broadcast live to the entire ship. We won't have long.' He gestured to Jax and Vanessa. 'Come here. Everyone should know the faces of the people who saved them.'

Much to Belinda's surprise, it was Vanessa who stepped forward first. 'Is this on?' she asked the Doctor. He nodded. She took a deep breath. 'For too long, we have worked on this cruise, with no reward, and no recognition. That ends today. By now, word has probably spread about Marilyn Moon's heinous plan to remove our memories. I know how scary the thought of that is. It nearly happened to me.' Her voice shook. 'There is an injustice taking place on board this ship right now. Throughout the lower decks, people are being held against their will. We were prisoners once, imprisoned for petty crimes, for getting in the way of those more powerful than us. But we have served our sentences. We cannot be held here for ever. Marilyn may try and claim that we've been brainwashed into saying this by the Moon Cruise Investigation, but that is impossible, when thousands of us have the same story, and none of us have ever left this ship.' Vanessa swayed a little on her feet, looking pale. Jax held her up, her face flushed with pride, her eyes sparkling.

'Keep going, V. You can do it.'

Vanessa nodded. 'We have detained Marilyn Moon. She no longer runs this cruise. We do. It is our responsibility now. On the upper decks, the stakeholders and investors are probably wondering what is going to happen to their profits. Keep them, we don't care. We just want our lives and our freedom back. We want to make something *new*. A new society, an equal one. Once, our blue jumpsuits were a uniform to be ashamed of. They made us remember how we'd been conned into giving up our every waking minute to serve Marilyn

Moon. But that is in the past. If you'll stand with me, these jumpsuits could be a badge of pride, worn by the citizens of our new society. A society that provides for everyone. That takes care of everyone. We need to transform this place into something new. A place to live and exist, a place where we can all be free.' She pressed a button on the keyboard and the broadcast ended.

There were a few moments of silence before, one by one, everybody started clapping.

'One more thing!' Belinda blurted out. The applause died down. 'The clone – Monroe – told me she had hidden a protocol inside every mannequin so control of them would revert back to her.'

The Doctor's eyes sparkled with mischief as he caught on to what she was saying. 'Go on.'

'What if we commandeered the protocol? We could give Jax and Vanessa control over the mannequins instead. You guys could turn them off for ever, or use them to help you take over the upper decks.' She shrugged. 'I don't think the stakeholders will be too happy that their cruise is being taken over. It might be handy to have some backup . . .'

When they finally left the workshop, Belinda was overjoyed to see the back of it.

'I can't wait to be in the TARDIS again,' she mused

as they trudged back towards the high-speed lift. 'It will seem like the lap of luxury after two days on this cruise.'

'I don't know if anyone has ever called the TARDIS luxurious before,' the Doctor laughed. 'But there's certainly a first time for everything.'

As they stepped inside the lift, Marilyn awoke. Ever since she had been hit with the memory gun, she kept dozing off, almost as if she had forgotten how to stay awake. She was draped over Jax's broad shoulder, limp and confused.

'W-what are you doing with me?' she slurred, clearly still groggy from the gun's effects. 'Where am I? *Who* am I?'

It turned out the memory ray was much stronger than Marilyn had let on. It had erased much more than the last seven years of her life. The Doctor had the gun now. Seeing what it had done to Marilyn had convinced them all that it should be taken off the ship and destroyed, as soon as possible.

Jax raised an eyebrow. 'Your name is Marilyn. You've led a simple life up until this point, just a regular person, with a regular job.'

'What was my job?'

Jax suppressed a smile. 'You worked in a souvenir shop, selling sunglasses.'

'... are you *sure*?' Marilyn sounded mystified.

Jax rolled her eyes. Leave it to Marilyn to still consider

herself above working in a shop, when she couldn't even remember her own name.

'Oh, positive,' Jax replied.

In the end, Belinda and the Doctor left Marilyn in the custody of Vanessa and Jax, who were being hailed as heroes. Word of their exploits had spread, and Vanessa's broadcast was already the stuff of legend. When they emerged from the lift, an enormous crowd had gathered to welcome them back. The mannequins were docile, vicious electric wires nowhere to be seen.

All around them were scenes of pure joy. People embracing, walking the concourses, mingling with passengers who had at first been scared, but as they had learned of everything that had been going on just out of sight, welcomed the crew members with open arms. She saw a bunch of former crew members heading for the beach – their jumpsuits pulled down to the waist, grabbing towels from the beach kiosk to sling around their shoulders. They whooped and laughed, joking around for the first time in years. Every single person that Belinda could see was as excited as a small child as they headed out to try all the activities they had been running for so long, but had never been afforded the opportunity to try for themselves.

She went to the balcony and looked out. After a while, the Doctor stood with her.

'I just remembered what the mystery of the Moon

Cruise was. The thing that spawned a thousand conspiracy theories once the cruise returned home.'

Belinda raised an eyebrow. 'Oh yeah?'

The Doctor crossed his arms. 'It was about Marilyn. She'll go down in history as one of the richest women to ever live. But, at the end of the cruise, she decided to donate every single penny she had to charity. She never explained why, and the Moon Cruise never sailed again.'

Belinda's eyes went wide. 'She donates the money?'

The Doctor grinned. 'Yep. And what does everyone say?'

Belinda laughed. 'I'll take a guess. Something like, "She must have been out of her mind."'

They both laughed, the tension of the last few days easing slightly.

'All in a good day's work,' the Doctor said, shaking his head. When Belinda didn't reply, he turned to her, grinning. 'You ready to head home? Or at least try to?'

Belinda sighed with bone-deep relief as she looped her arm through his, walking back towards the blue police box. 'I thought you'd never ask.'

The last thing they saw before they ducked into the service corridor, scooped up the Vindicator and left the Moon Cruise for good, was Jax and Vanessa. They had escaped the crowds and were walking through the concourse, talking quietly, their heads bent together.

Soon, they found a quiet place to be alone, next to one of the enormous windows. For many moments, they didn't speak. They just looked out into the vastness of space. Then Vanessa leaned her head against Jax's shoulder, and Jax rested her head on Vanessa's, their fingers intertwining as they stared out at the stars, finally together.

Acknowledgements

My sincerest thanks to everyone involved in making this book a reality; Steve Cole—editor extraordinaire, it has been so wonderful to work with you, as always. James Page—what on earth would we do without you? Thank you of course to everyone at Penguin; thank you to Shammah Banerjee for thinking of me for this project, and Clementine Lussiana for keeping us on track. Thank you to the rest of the team; Percie Bridgewater, and Albert DePetrillo. And an enormous thank you as always to my truly incredible agent Catherine Cho, and to the team at Paper Literary for your support.

Lastly, but most importantly of all, thank you to the Doctor Who readers, who are consistently the kindest and funniest in any signing line. I am very grateful for the chance to add an original story to the Doctor's vast universe.